Murder on a Hitman's Trail

Book Three

By Robert D. Coleman

MURDER ON A HITMAN'S TRAIL, BOOK THREE

First edition. September 7, 2019.

Copyright © 2019 Robert D. Coleman.

ISBN: 979-8224580217

Written by Robert D. Coleman.

Chapter 1

John Carter heard his alarm going off. He considered hitting the snooze button a 2nd time. He rolled over to find that Carolyn was already up and in the bathroom. He laid there on his back and looked at the ceiling. He didn't really want to start another day.

The last two months have been really hard. The fire destroying Fort Parker. The killer of all those people getting away. That last chilling phone call he made from Doyle McKinney's phone. Then finding McKinney dead. He knew McKinney was the money behind the murders. All the people killed were people that had something to do with his son going to jail on drug charges. What he did not know is what happened to make the killer turn on McKinney.

The case had gone cold. He had gotten clean away. He had shared what little evidence he had over to the FBI office in Waco. He had hoped that they could enhance the photo that was taken of the man after he shot the Police officer in Mart and run it through there facial recognition software. But so far nothing.

The people of Groesbeck and Limestone County had lost a lot of respect for him. His re-election was no longer a sure thing. When last he checked his poll numbers were way down. He could understand why the people had lost faith in him. He had made a huge mistake not calling in the FBI sooner. It all had just snowballed so fast.

He wished he could go back and fix it. But he couldn't. The only thing he could do was keep looking. Keep working every angle and find that son of a bitch. Then if that was it and he lost re-election. Then so be it. But he owed it to all the people that died. To give it his all!

He threw the cover back and got up out of bed. He reached and put his robe on and turned and walked toward the bathroom. As he got to the door he met Carolyn coming out. He looked at her and smiled. "Morning." He said. She looked back at him and didn't return the smile and said. "Can you take the kids to school today? I'm going in to work early today. Maybe if I get there before anybody else I might sell something today." He nodded his head. "Sure babe." She moved to walk by him. He reached to try to kiss her, but she quickly moved passed him. When she got to the door he said. "Things are going to get better Babe. It's just going to take a little time." She stops and looks back at him. "Really John. It's all about sales, and I have none! My reputation is damaged to the point I'm not likely to get any. That means no commissions. No money for our family. Better yet no money for my company. I have been lucky. They have stood by me so far. Hoping this will all blow over. But that's not going to last forever. So things need to get better fast." She takes a long look at him and tries to force a small smile.

Carter watches as she walks out of the bedroom. He walks into the bathroom and looks in the mirror. She was right. Everything she said. Only it was not her fault. She was guilty by association. Her name was Carter. It was his fault. He had to somehow make this right. He didn't want his family to suffer because of him.

He quickly showered and shaved and got dressed. Pulling on his cowboy boots and buttoning up his white work shirt. He walked over to the dresser and took out his wallet. He removed his badge and put the wallet in his back pocket. He then pinned the badge to the left side of his shirt. He put on his gun belt and walked over to his safe. He hit the six-digit code and it opened. Taking out his 38 revolver. He took a long look at it as he took it out. It had J.D.C. on the butt. It had been his Papaw's gun. He had been sheriff of neighboring Freestone County for 20 years. He wondered what his Papaw would think of him now. He checked the load and put it in his holster.

He turned and walked out of the bedroom and headed to the kitchen. When he got there, he found no coffee going. That was not good. He could really use a cup.

He then heard Becky beating on the bathroom door and yelling at her brother. Ok, coffee would have to wait. He walked down the hall to where she was standing outside the bathroom door. She looked over at him and said. "Daddy Tom's in the bathroom and won't come out!" Carter looks at her and says. "Just use your mother's bathroom." She looks back at him. "All my makeup and stuff are in here!" Carter then knocks on the door. He can then hear Tom singing in there. "Taking care of business every day. Taking care of business every way. Taking care of business." Carter then yells through the door. "Tom, what are you doing in there?" There was a long pause. Tom then said. "I'm taking care of business, Dad." Carter then says. "Well, hurry it up. Your sister needs to get in there." Tom then says back. "Ok, Dad. Just finishing up the paperwork now." Carter then turns and walks back toward the kitchen. A moment later, the door opens, and Tom walks out. He puts a pair of sunglasses on, looks his sister in the eye, and says. "And working overtime."

She hurried past him in the bathroom. A moment later, she came back out with a frown on her face. She yelled, "Oh my gosh, Tom! Really!"

Back in the kitchen Carter turns and looks at Tom. "Looks like we are on our own for breakfast." Tom walks past him and says. "Looks like its a pop tart morning." He walks past his Dad and gets into the pantry and pulls out a box of pop tarts. He opens the package and puts them in the toaster. Carter then says. "I can fix you up some eggs and toast?" "Naw Dad. I'm good." Becky then walks out into the kitchen. Gives Tom a dirty look. He smiles back at her. Carter looks over at her. "You want some eggs and toast?" She looks over at him and smiles. "No Daddy. Thank you. I will just grab some yogurt." She reaches in the fridge and pulls some out and grabs a spoon.

They all sat down at the table. Carter looks over at Becky and says. "Isn't it about time for the drama club to put on another play?" She looks back over at him and says. "Yes, Daddy." He smiles at her big.

"So you have a bigger speaking part this time?" She looks down at her yogurt. "No Daddy. I didn't get a part." He looks over at her. "Really. You were the only freshman with a speaking part last time." She looks up. "I was just lucky I guess." He smiles at her. "I'm sure it will work out better next time. Hang in there. Keep working hard at it." She nods her head and stands up and throws her empty yogurt in the trash.

Carter stands up. "Well, I guess we better get going. They all start walking toward the front door. Carter grabs his Silver belly cowboy hat and puts it on his head as he walks out the door.

Outside, Carter looks over and sees a pile of his re-election signs lying in the yard. Tom looks at the signs and says, "Why do they keep picking up our signs and throwing them out in the yard?" Carter starts walking toward the car. "It's okay, son. We'll get them put back out. Don't worry about it now."

The kids get in his squad car and they head off to school. Carter stops at a convenience store. He really needs a good cup of coffee. Carter stops and says to the kids. I'm going to grab some coffee. He gets out and walks up to the door. There is a boy about Tom's age standing at the door. Carter looks at him and says. "Good morning. How are you today?" The boy looks at him with a sad look on his face. He nods but doesn't speak. Carter opens the door and goes inside. He sees Bill Curry leaving the counter and heading to the door. "Hey, morning Bill. How's it going?" Bill looks at Carter and walks by without saying anything. Carter stops and watches him, walk out. Wow has it come to this. People I have known for years don't even speak anymore. He walks over and gets his coffee and checks out.

Carter gets back in the car and makes the short drive to the High School and pulls up to the front. Becky reaches over and gives him a kiss on the cheek. "Bye Daddy. Love you." Carter smiles "Love you too sweetheart." Tom then says. "Can you let me out at the other end please?" Carter glances toward the back seat. "Ya, I guess so. Why?" Tom leans forward putting his fingers through the screen the separates the front form the back seats. "Because that's where all the babe's hang out!"

Carter drives down to the other end, gets out, and opens the back door. Tom gets out and looks over at the girls standing on the top of the steps. He puts his sunglasses on and says, "These are my people!" He gives his Dad a big smile. "Later, Dad." Carter smiles as he gets back in the car.

He then pulled out and headed to the office. He had hoped that things would be getting back to normal by now. But it didn't look like that was going to happen. People were taking his signs down, and friends were not talking to him, not to mention the problem with Carolyn and her job. He was trying hard not to get discouraged.

Pulling up at the Sheriff's Department, he got out and walked inside. The first person he saw was his secretary, Nancy Hall. She looked over at him. "Are we working bankers, hours now?" He smiled at her. "No, I had to take the kids to school today."

He walks into his office and sets down at his desk. A moment later Nancy comes in and hands him a cup of Coffee she has poured for him. Taking the cup. "Thank you, Nancy." "How are you doing this morning?" She asks. He looks up at her. "I have had better mornings." She turns to walk away and says. "Well drink your coffee. I'm sure that will make it better." He smiles at her as she walks out. He takes a big sip of the coffee. He then frowns. I wouldn't bet on that.

His Chief Deputy Greg Roberts Walks in with a hand full of papers. He says. "Morning Sheriff. Have you had your coffee yet?" Carter looks at him. "I had a fair cup on the way to work. I just started on Nancy's coffee. So I don't see my mood getting any better.

Roberts hands him the papers he was carrying. Carter looks at the papers and then looks up at Roberts. "Mike Tully Is resigning? He has been with me for years." Roberts looks over at Carter. "Yes apparently so." Carter puts the papers down on his desk. "Is he here?"

"Yes," Roberts replies. "Ask him to come in here please." Roberts turns and walks out. A minute later Deputy Mike Tully walks in.

"Good morning Mike," Carter says. "Have a seat." Deputy Tully sets down. Carter then holds up the resignation papers. "I just received this. To be honest. I was surprised. We have been together for years. You haven't said anything about wanting to leave." Tully looks up at Carter. "Well, Sheriff its something I have been thinking about for some time now. I just didn't want to say anything till I was sure." Carter nods his head and sets down in his chair. "Have you got another job?" Tully then lowers his head. "No, not right now. But I'm sure I will find something. It was just time for a change."

Both men stand up, and Carter walks around his desk. Carter offers his hand to Tully. "If there is anything I can do to help, just let me know." The two men shake hands, and Tully says, "Thank you, Sheriff." Tully turns and walks out.

A moment later Roberts walks back in. Carter looks over at him and says. "Now that was kinda strange. He ups and leaves a job he has had for years. Without having another job. Just because it's time for a change? Got to be more to it than that." Roberts turns and closes the door and comes back.

"Well, there has been some talk," Roberts says. Both men sit down. "I have heard that Tully is going to endorse James Wright for Sheriff. Hoping that if he wins, with his experience he will get his job back. Maybe even Chief Deputy." Carter sets back in his chair. "He is afraid if he says on with me and Wright wins. He will clean house and he will be out of a job." Carter looks over at Roberts. "I never thought about it that way. Probably because I never really thought about losing." "Well, " Roberts says. "I think it's really disrespectful. After everything you have done for him." Carter leaned forward in his chair. "Well. I am a little hurt. But the man has a family to think of." Roberts stands up. "When you're re-elected. He is going to regret this." Carter smiles. "Well see."

Roberts turns and walks out. Carter sets back in his chair and takes another sip of his coffee. He wonders how many other deputies will follow Tully's lead and leave. They were already short-handed. Things seem to be going from bad to worse.

Chapter 2

Jake Slone jerked awake. He had fallen asleep watching the small TV. He stood up and looked outside. It was dark. He pulled his phone out and checked the time. It was 9:20 pm. He must have slept for about an hour.

He walked to the other end of his small travel trailer. He opened the small refrigerator. Looking inside he saw no beer, no soda, no tea, no water. He closed the door and let out a loud sigh. He was thirsty and it looked like he was out of luck.

He walked back to the bedroom and put on his boots. There was a convenience store right down the street. He would walk down there to get something to drink and get some fresh air. He started to pick up his 9mm pistol, but then he put it down. It was too hard to conceal, and he was not going to be gone long.

He stepped outside. It had started to cool down now that the sun was down. He locked the trailer he had been staying in the last few months. It was small but it served his needs. He had found a cheap place to park it in Broken Arrow Oklahoma. A city of about 100,000 people or so. Not too small but not too big. A good place for him to lay low and it was only about 20 miles from Tusla. Were his Mom and 10-year-old daughter Michelle lived. She had just had a birthday that he had missed. He hated to disappoint her. His life had been a mess in the last few months. He had taken that job he shouldn't have taken. But he had needed the money. Michelle had been very sick with heart problems. He had not worked in 8 months after coming home from Afghanistan. He needed to work. Michelle needed treatment and he had no Insurance. So he took a job close to home. Big mistake. Now here he was hiding out and afraid to go back home. He tried to keep in touch with his Mom to keep track of how Michelle was doing. But it was not the same as being there.

He slowly made the walk down to the convenience store, keeping a lookout for anything that could be a problem. He stopped across the street and took a long look around. He wanted to know everything going on around the store before walking in, including where the cameras were, everything. He couldn't take any chances.

Pulling his cap down low, he headed to the door, looking down and away every time he came in view of a camera. He opened the door and walked in. The clerk spoke as he came in. "Hey, how are you tonight?" Slone turned his head away and said, "Fine, thank you."

As he walked down the aisle toward the cooler in the back, he passed a young, very good-looking girl walking toward the counter. He smiled at her, and she returned the smile. He walked down to the soda door. He looked inside and quickly found what he wanted. He opened the door and took out a soda bottle.

About that time he heard the front doorbell go off. He turned to see three rough-looking men walk in. They all gave the young girl at the counter a long look. One of them looked at her and said. "Hey, baby." She looked at him and said. "Hello." She quickly paid for her stuff and turns for the door. He looks at her and says. "We need to get to know each other." She moves toward the door fast and says. "I'm in a hurry." She opens the door and goes outside.

All the while, the other two guys are picking up stuff and putting it in a bag. The first guy walks behind the counter. The clerk says, "Please, Hector, not again." He looks at the clerk. "Stop your crying. We just take what we want, and we will be gone, and you get to keep breathing." He turns and grabs two packs of cigarettes. "Let's go, " he says. The man called Hector and the two others walk out the door.

Slone walks up to the counter and pays for his soda. He looks at the clerk. "That happens a lot?" "Yes." the clerk says. Slone looks at him. "Call the police." The clerk looks back at him. "It won't do any good. It will just piss him off. My boss just wants to let it go. As long as nobody gets hurt." Slone turns and walks toward the door and stops and turns and looks at the clerk. "You keep letting it go and sooner or later somebody will get hurt!"

He opens the door and walks out. He can see the young girl walking down the street a block or so away. He can also see the Hector and his two guys walking half a block behind her. He thought to himself. It was none of his business. It was in the wrong direction from his trailer. "Aw hell." He said as he turned to walk toward them.

He watched as the girl turned and walked down an ally. Aw, big mistake girl. He thought as he hurried to catch up. When he turned to go down the ally he saw Hector and his boys had backed the girl up to the side of a building. They didn't even look up as he walked toward them. He stopped about 10 yards away from them and said. "Hey, guys. Why don't you just make it easy on yourself and let the girl go! We can go our separate ways and nobody has to get hurt." Hector who had the girl pinned to the wall and his two men turn and look at Slone. "Who the fuck are you old man? You better get your ass out of here while you still can. Slone pulls his bottle of soda out and opens it and takes a long drink. He puts the cap back on the bottle and says. "I'm am the old man that's going to kick your ass if you don't do what I say." Hector looks back at him and says. "Do you know who I am?" Slone takes another drink from his soda and looks back. "I don't give a fuck who you are!" Hector looks over at his men. "Get rid of this bum." The two men start moving toward him. Slone quickly moves up and hits the first one hard in the face. He swings around and kicks high hitting the 2nd man in the jaw with his boot knocking him to the ground. He then comes back to the 1st one with a hard right to the jaw he bends over and Slone comes down hard with an elbow.

With the two men on the ground, he starts toward Hector. Hector turns and pulls a knife and says. "Ok, I'm going to cut you into little pieces." He comes toward Slone and takes a swing with his knife. Slone quickly moves out of the way and comes across with a hard left to the face. Hector staggers back and then comes forward swinging the knife again and again missing. Slone then grabs the arm with the knife and twists his arm, forcing him to drop the knife. He then grabs Hector's right thumb and twists. Hector cries out in pain. Slone smiles. "That hurts, doesn't it? See, I have dislocated your thumb. A lot of nerves in your hands. Very painful. You see if I put just a little more pressure on it. The bone will pop right threw. Now get on your knees." He pressed harder, and Hector did as he was told and got on his knees. "Ok. You're going to stay away from that store, and you're going to leave that girl alone! Understood?" Hector nods his head. Slone then hits him hard in the face and lets him go as he falls to the ground.

Slone then looks over at the girl. "Are you okay?" She nods her head and says, "Yes." Slone then walks toward her and says, "Ok, you need to get gone then. It's not safe to be out in this area this late." She turns to walk away, stops, and looks at Slone. "Thank you." She then turns and hurryes off.

Slone then walks around and picks up the stuff they stole from the store and puts it all in a bag. He then walks back over to Hector and rolls him over. Takes out his wallet and takes a 20 dollar bill out. He throws the wallet back down. He reaches down and grabs Hector by the hair and pulls his head up and slaps him lightly on the jaw. "Hey, I'm taking 20 dollars for the two packs of cigarettes you opened and smoked." He then wiggled Hector's nose. He winced in pain. "Ya, I'm thinking that nose is broken. I would get some ice for that." As he picked up the bag and started to walk off the first guy was starting to get up. He hit him over the head with his elbow. He fell back to the ground.

He walked out of the alley and back to the convenience store. He walked up to the door and tapped on it, holding the bag with the stolen stuff and the 20 dollars in it so the clerk could see it. When he opened the door, he handed it to him. He turned and walked away without saying anything. The confused-looking clerk walked back inside.

Slone turned and started walking back toward the trailer. He shook his head. Now, he was going to have to move. Damn, why couldn't he have just minded his own business. Hector didn't seem the type to just let this go.

When he returned to the trailer, he slept for a few hours, then got up and started getting ready to move. He tried to move every few weeks anyway. As he started the truck and pulled out, he headed to the next spot he had already planned to move to.

He pulled into the trailer park and paid for his spot for a few weeks. He spent the next few hours setting everything up. He set down in his desk chair. Damn still no soda. He laughed and looked over at the picture that had been turned down for the move. He picked it up and looked at it. It was a picture of Mitchelle taken right before they found out about her heart problems. She had a big smile on her face. She looked so happy. He picked up the other picture on the desk. It was of Him and Michelle and her mother Jessica it was taken when Michelle was a baby. They had just gotten married. They were both in there Navy dress uniforms. They were so happy. They were both fixing to deploy out to Afghanistan. Michelle was going to stay with his mom for a few months until Jessica's commitment to the Navy was up. He was planning to make the Navy a career. He was part of a Navy Seal team. He had just made the rank of Lieutenant Commander.

What had happened to his life? Jessica was dead. Michelle was sick. Most people thought he was dead. And he probably soon would be. How had things gone so wrong?

A few hours later, he got in his truck and drove the 30 miles across town to his mother's place. He drove by the house slowly. They were home. He took a long look at the place, hoping to catch a glimpse of Michelle. He then drove to a nearby park and waited for it to get dark.

When dark came, he drove back to the house. He parked about a block away and walked to the house. He could see lights on inside. He knew he shouldn't, but he couldn't help himself. He walked up to a window and peeked inside. I could see Michelle sitting on the couch, wrapped up in a blanket. She looked thin and pale. After taking a long look, he walked over to the birdbath in the yard. There was a statue sitting in it. He moved it and turned it to face north. He knew his mother would check it before she went to bed. He then drove back to the park and waited.

About 45 minutes later, he saw his mother's car drive up, and she got out and walked over to the bench under the light. He waited a few minutes to see if she had been followed. He then walked over to her. "He,y Mom." He said as he walked up. She stood up, smiled, and hugged him. "Oh, Jake. It's good to see you." He smiled, and they sat down. Slone reached out and held her hand. "How is she, Mom?" She gave him a worried look and said. "She is getting weaker. Her doctors have said a transplant is her best option. She is on the list, but it will take time." He looked down, and then he looked back up at her. "Time she may not have," he said. She squeezed his hand. "You don't know that, Jake." He turned his head to look at her. "I know I have to do something." He stood up and turned to face her. "I'm going to take care of this. I will figure something out." She stood up. He took both hands and cupped her face and wiped away a tear. He then kissed her on the forehead. "Take care of her, Mom." She shook her head and said. "Of Course."

He turned and walked away. Somehow, he had to fix this even if it meant selling his soul again.

Chapter 3

John Carter sat at his desk and tried to get some work done. But he was not having much luck. Everything kept coming back through his mind. He had gotten a call from County Commissioner Jessie Cortez. He and Mayor Bobby Bozeman Wanted to meet with him at the Courthouse this morning. He really didn't want to go. He and Commissioner Cortez had been friends for years, but his relationship with Mayor Bozeman had been strained at best.

He closed the file on his desk and got up and walked through the door out in the bullpen. He saw Deputy Roberts and walked over to him. "Hey, Greg. I'm on my way over to the Courthouse to meet with Cortez and Bozeman. Hold down the fort while I'm gone." Roberts looks over at him and says. "Will do, boss. Got any idea what this is all about?" Carter shakes his head. "No idea. Hopefully, it won't take long."

Carter turns and walks out to the parking lot, gets in his car, and makes the short drive to the Courthouse.

Inside, he walks down to the Commissioner's meeting room and walks inside. He finds Commissioner Cortez and Mayor Bozeman waiting for him. Mayor Bozeman walks toward him, and they shake hands. "Thank you for Coming, Sheriff." Carter then turns to Cortez, who looks at him, smiles, and offers his hand. Carter shakes his hand. Cortez says, "It's good to see you, John. Thanks for coming. I know you're busy."

Bozeman pulls a chair out and says, "Have a seat, Sheriff. This won't take long." The three men set down. Carter looks over at them and says, "What can I do for you, gentlemen?"

Commissioner Cortez looks down and away. Carter recognizes that from years of interrogating suspects. He knows what this is about and doesn't want to be here. Mayor Bozeman, on the other hand, is making eye contact and looked confident, almost eager, to get this started. This was Bozeman's show. He would do most of the talking. Cortez was just here as a show of support. He probably had drawn the short straw among the Commissioners.

Bozeman then spoke up. "Sheriff, with the election only a few months away. There are some things that we are concerned about. Mainly your poll numbers. They have fallen like a rock for the last few months. From a high of 74% a few months ago. Right after your Republican Primary win to 28% a few days ago. I feel like this clearly shows that the public has lost confidence in you and your handling of the murders that have rocked our beloved city and County. So what we propose for the good of the County is your resign and drop out of the election. You can say it's for health reasons or family reasons or whatever you want. Then we can name a replacement. Somebody totally from the outside, not connected to your office in any way. Then maybe, just mayb,e we will have a fighting chance against Democrat James Wright. So what do you say, John? Will you help us out?

There was an awkward silence for a moment as Carter stared at Bozeman. He then looked over at Cortez, who still was not making eye contact. He looked back at Bozeman. "Let me get this straight. You're the Mayor of Groesbeck, who has no authority over me, the elected County Sheriff. You're asking me for my resignation?"

After another moment of awkward silence, Bozeman said, "Yes, Sheriff, that's what I'm asking. I might add that I'm on the election ballot, too, and you are dragging me and all the other Republicans down, too. And as I'm sure you have noticed, County Commissioner Cortez is with me, and he does have authority over you!"

Carter looks over at Cortez. "Is that what the Commissioners are asking?" Cortez forces himself to make eye contact. "There has been some talk. There is some concern about your dropping poll numbers. But no vote has been taken." He looks over at Bozeman. It was my understanding that this meeting was to talk to you about ways we could get your poll numbers up and to find out how you felt about things. If you even wanted to stay on after everything that has happened.

"Oh, ok," Carter said. "I will take what you have said under consideration. It has been tough on my family. I will let you know as soon as I can. I just need some time to think and talk to my family."

Carter stands up as do the other men. He offers his hand to Cortez. Cortez takes his hand. "Thank you, John." He says. Carter looks over at Bozeman. They make eye contact. Carter nods and says. "Mayor." Carter turns and walks out the door.

As Carter slowly walks through the Courthouse. Maybe it should do what they want. It was clear that he had lost a lot of support. Even his own staff were turning on him. Maybe a fresh start someplace else would be a good thing.

Carter then noticed a lot of commotion going on. A lot of people running around. Carter quickly snapped out of his daze. He saw a security guard run by. "What's going on?" Carter shouted at the guard. He looked over at Carter. Seeing who he was he quickly stopped. "There is a kid up on the roof. Threatening to jump.

Carter looks at the guard. "You're with me." He turns and heads for the stairs. They hurry up two flights of stairs. On the way up, Carter pulls out his cell phone and calls Deputy Roberts. Roberts answers. "Hey, Sheriff," Carter says. "We got a kid on the roof here at the Courthouse." "Ya, we know," Roberts says. "Hayes and I are on our way." "Good, " Carter says. "I will be on the roof." Carter hangs up and puts his phone away just as they get to the top of the stairs.

Carter looks over at the guard. "How do we get to the roof?" The guard turns and says. "This way." They walk down the side of one of the courtrooms, and there is a door, inside is a ladder. Carter looks over at the guard. "The door wasn't locked? Please tell me it's not that easy to get up there!" The guard looks at him. "It's supposed to stay locked." Carter starts climbing. "Well, obviously it wasn't!"

Walking out on the roof, Carter looks around and sees the boy standing on the other side of the rail on the ledge. Carter slowly starts walking toward the boy. He turns around and sees Carter. "Stop. Don't come any closer, " the boy says. Carter stops walking and says, "Ok. I just want to talk to you. My name is Sheriff John Carter. What's yours?"

The boys turned and looked down and then back to Carter. "Steven, Steven Smith." Carter nodded and moved a few steps closer. "Ok, Steven. Is there something I can help you with? Why don't you come back over on this side, and we will go inside and talk."

Steven looked over at Carter and said, "No, I don't want to talk! Talking just makes me think about it, and all I want to do is forget! Tell those people on the ground to get back." Carter then said, "Ok. I'm going to get word to them right now. So just say calm."

Carter turns to see Deputies Roberts and Hayes standing just inside the door on the roof. He walks back to them. Roberts hands Carter an earbud, and Carter puts it in his ear. Now, they will be able to hear everything that Carter says. Carter turns and looks at Hayes. The kid's name is Steven Smith. Call his parents and get me everything you can on him. And tell the guys on the ground to get back." Hayes turns to leave and says. "I'm on it." Carter turns to Roberts. "You stay right here. I may need you."

Carter turns and starts walking back toward Steven. He gets to about the spot where he was before. "Hey, Steven. I sent word down for them to get back." Steven turns to him and says, "Ok. Thank you." Carter takes a few steps forward. "Can I come a little bit closer? Make it easier for us to talk?" Steven turns and says, "Ya, but not too close."

Carter moved up to the rail but was still a good 10 feet away. "So, Steven. Didn't I run into you this morning down at the store by the school?" Steven looks down. "Ya, that was me." Carter smiles. "I thought that was you. I was taking my kids to school. You probably know them. Tom and Becky Carter? Steven shook his head. "Ya, I know, Tom We have a few classes together. I don't know Becky that well."

Ok, good Carter thought. Maybe that would give us something to talk to him about. "Ya, I got my hands full with that boy Tom, I tell ya." Steven smiled.

"So Steven, is there anybody that I can call for you?" Maybe your parents? There was a long pause. Steven said nothing. Then, he heard Deputy Hayes talking in his ear. "Hey, boss. Checking on this kid. Both parents are dead. His father, Steven Smith Sr. killed in Afghanistan two years ago. His mother was Pam Smith. She was one of the victims a few months ago." Carter's heart sank. What this kid must have been through. He was probably the last person that needed to be talking to this kid.

About that time, Steven turned and said. "I don't have any parents anymore." Carter turned to look at Steven. "I'm so sorry about that. I can only imagine how hard that is. But you can't give up. You have to hang in there. Be strong. You will get through it. Your parents wouldn't want you to do this, son."

Steven looked over at Carter. "I'm the one that found my mother! I can't get that picture out of my head." Carter inched closer to the boy. "I know that's got to be the worst thing you can go through. I want to help you. Take my hand, and let's go inside and talk." Steven shook his head hard. "No!"

Carter threw his legs over the rail and stood on the 18-inch ledge. Steven looked hard at him. "What are you doing? Stay back." Carter turned to him. "I'm not getting any closer. But if we can't talk inside, we will have to talk here." Steven looks down. "I don't want to talk." Carter inched a little closer. "Ok, you don't have to talk. So I will talk, and you just listen. Your Mom's case is still open. I'm still working on it. And I'm going to keep working on it. I'm not going to give up! I promise you that I will work on it as long as I am physically able. I just need you to give me some time. I need you to believe in me. I won't let you down."

Carter moved closer to the boy. His foot slipped, and he fell to a knee. Steven reached out and grabbed him, pulling him up. Carter then reached around the boy in a bear hug, grabbed the rail behind him, and held on tight.

Deputy Roberts and Hayes, watching from the roof door, ran over, grabbed Steven, and pulled him back over the rail. Carter then climbed over. Steven looks at him with tears in his eyes. "You tricked me." Carter walks over to him and puts his hand on his shoulder. "I did what I had to do, son. But I meant what I said. I'm going to get you some help, and I'm going to keep working on your Mom's case for as long as it takes. You have my word on that. I will keep you updated on how it's going. Ok?" Steven shakes his head as Robert leads him away.

Carter then heads down the ladder and stairs to the lobby of the Courthouse. He sees Commissioner Cortez and Mayor Bozeman. He walks over to them. Bozeman says. "Well, I'm glad that worked out, Sheriff. That would have been even more bad press. We sure don't need that." Carter takes a hard look at him. In a loud voice says. "It would have been kinda bad for the kids, too!" Bozeman's eyes got big, andhe says. "Oh, well." Carter puts his hand up and stops him. "Just stop. Don't say anymore, please!" Carter then looks over at Cortez. "You can tell the Commissioners and anybody else that wants to know. I won't quit! Not now. Not ever!"

Carter turns and walks toward the door, meeting Roberts and Hayes. He looks at them and says. "Ok, we are done waiting for some kind of break on this case. We are going to see Mike McKinney in prison. We are going to rattle his cage until he gives us something on his Dad!

I made a promise to that boy, and I'm going to keep it!

Chapter 4

Jake Slone abruptly woke up. He had slept very deeply. He was sure he needed the rest. But he hated sleeping like that. In his line of work, it could get him killed.

He got up and got in the shower. One of the things he hated about living in a travel trailer was the size of the shower. Getting out and drying off, he looked in the mirror. Did he even know the man looking back? He needed a haircut. It was touching the top of his ears. His beard and mustache also needed trimming badly. He would stop this morning and get a haircut and trim. When he met Hunter today, he didn't want to look like a bum. Nathan Hunter had been his friend, mentor, and boss for around 10 years now. He had messed up last year taking that job without going through Hunter. That had been a mistake. One he wouldn't make again. If there was anybody he could count on, it was Nathan Hunter.

He quickly got dressed. Pulling on a tee-shirt, he pulled the shirttail out to cover his 9mm pistol under his belt. He didn't think he would need it, but he would rather have it and not need it than not have it and need it.

He grabbed a cup of coffee as he went out the door, got in the pickup, and drove around the corner to a barber shop. They were just about to open, and he was the first customer of the day. He told the man he wanted a shortcut and a beard trim.

As the barber started to cut, he could hear the man talking, but he was only half-listening. He was thinking about Mitchelle, what that poor girl had been through in her short life.

He had met her mother, Jessica, in Afghanistan. They were both in the Navy. He was a Lieutenant Commander and team leader of Seal

Team 10. She was a helicopter pilot. She dropped off and picked up his team on most of their missions.

They had worked together for a year before they got involved. For obvious reasons, the Navy did not like people who worked together getting involved romantically, so they had to keep it a secret. They were very much in love, but both of them were shocked when she became pregnant.

Jessica had no family. So after a few months, she was sent home for the birth of her child. She went back to Tulsa, Oklahom,a and stayed with his mother. When it got close to the time of birth, he got to come home for a while.

Mitchelle was born and happy. He and Jessica got married soon after. They didn't tell the Navy. He soon returned to Afghanistan, and she came back a month later. She only had six months until her time in the Navy was up. He was going to stay in and make the Navy a career. He loved the Navy. He hoped to become a Seal instructor so he would be stationed stateside.

About that time, the barber said something to him that brought him out of his thoughts. He held up a mirror and asked if it looked okay. "Yes, that's good," Slone said, taking a long look in the mirror. Yes, it's much better. His hair and beard look good.

The barber took the cover off from around his neck and brushed away any loose hair. Slone got up and walked to the counter and paid. The man handed back his change. Slone looked at him and said. "Thank you. Have a great day."

Slone walked to his truck, drove down the street, and made one more stop at a flower shop. As he opened the door to go in, a cowbell that was attached to the door went off. Inside, a strong smell of flowers overwhelmed the room. A young girl walked out of the backroom and smiled at him. "Can I help you?" Slone smiled back. "I need a dozen roses." She looked over at him. "What color would you like, sir?" Slone thought for a moment. "Red, and could I get a glass vase, please?" She smiled and said. "Yes, sir. I will be right back."

He looked around for a moment while the girl went into the backroom. He didn't remember the last time he had bought flowers. The girl came back out with beautiful red roses in a lovely vase. "Will there be anything else?" The girl asks. "No, that will be it." She rang him u,p and he paid her in cash. She handed him back his change. He picked up his flowers and smiled at her. "Thank you very much. You have a great day." The girl smiled back and said. "Thank you. You too, sir."

He got in the truck and drove down the road. He had one more stop to make before his meeting. He pulled into the parking lot and looked around. He wanted to make sure there were no cameras.

He had been meaning to come here for the last year that he had been home. But he just hadn't done it. Not that he didn't want to. It was just knowing what memories it would bring back.

He got out. He took out his roses and walked up to the main gate that said. Memorial Park Cemetery. Inside, he looked around. He had a lot of family here. He stopped at his father's grave and looked down. Richard D. Slone, he had died of cancer when he was in High School. He had been a good husband, father, and man of God. He lowered his head. "I'm sorry I have let you down, Dad. I know how ashamed of me you must be!"

He walked down a few more plots till he came to the one he came here to see. He knelt down and placed the flower at the headstone. It read Jessica D. Slone, his wife. As he looked at it, tears started coming down his face. "I'm so sorry, Jess. I have let you and Mitchelle down so badly! I know that you can never forgive me for what I have done. I'm going to do everything I can to help Mitchelle. You have my word on that!" He placed the roses in a holder next to the headstone.

He looked over at the headstone next to hers. He got an eerie feeling as he read his own name on it. Jake A. Slone. He looked at the date of death. It was 3 days after her's. Those were 3 days he would never forget!

*

(10 years earlier. Afghanistan)

Slone had been tossing and turning the last few hours. He was finally relieved to hear the phone ring. He grabbed the phone. "Commander Slone." "It's a go!" The voice on the other end said. "Understood," Slone said.

He sat up in his bed and called out to his roommate, Sargent Jim Dorsey. "Hey, Jimbo, Get up. It's a go!"

Dorsey and Slone had been friends for years. They went to school together in Tulsa, Oklahoma, and joined the Navy together right out of high school. They both got accepted to the SEAL program.

Dorsey set up. "I'm awake. Not like it could sleep with all the turning you did all night." Slone stood up and started toward the bathroom. "Ya ya Well, you were snoring. Go get everybody up. We are out of here in 45 minutes."

Thirty minutes later, all the members of Alfa, Bravo, and Charlie teams were out front, ready to go with all their stuff. Slone did a quick count and had all of his Alfa Team. He then shouted, "Alfa team all present and accounted for." Bravo team leader then said. "Bravo team, all present and accounted for," followed by Charlie team leader. "Charlie team all present and accounted for." Slone the shouted. "Everybody on the truck, and let's move out!"

They all got on the truck and made a quick trip to the hanger. They got out, went inside, and gathered around a large map.

Everybody settled down and got quiet. Slone walked up to the map and looked back at the three 8-man teams. "Ok, we have good intel that a high-value target is at this location. So, let's go over this one more time. The H.V.T. name is Omar Alead. He pointed to the picture of him on the wall. He is the number 3 man in Al Qaeda.

We believe he is held up in this compound. Each team will leave by helicopter. Alfa team will breach from the front, and Bravo team will breach from the back. We expect them to be armed and to put up a fight. We also believe that there may be women and children in the compound. We will try to keep collateral damage to a minimum. But they may use them as human shields. Charlie team will be 15 minutes behind us. They will reinforce where needed or help with the mop-up. Any questions?" Slone waited a moment. When nobody spoke up, he then said. "We leave in 30 Minutes.

Slone walked back to the office and got all his equipment ready. A few minutes later, Sargent Dorsey Walks in. He looks over at Slone and says. "When will Charlie Team get something other than mop-up duty?" Slone smiles. "Well, when your guys get more time in. They will get to rotate in." Dorsey raises his arms up and back down. "Ok, where does that leave me?" Slone shakes his head. "Well, somebody has to lead the team." Slone walks over and sits down at the small desk. "This is the night we are going to get Alead! I bet you get more than mop up." Dorsey smiles. "I hope you are right. This guy has been like a ghost. Every time we get close, he is gone."

Dorsey turns to walk out when Slone says. "Have the pilots made it yet?" Dorsey turns and looks back and smiles as he reaches the door. "Yes, they are here. Down at the other end of the hanger getting ready."

Slone followed Dorsey out the door and walked down to the end of the hanger, where the pilots were getting ready. As he walked up, he made eye contact with Jessica. She tried not to smile when she saw him. But she couldn't help herself. Slone walked out the end of the hanger, and a few moments later, she followed. They had not seen each other in a few days. He wanted to hug and kiss her, but he knew they could not risk it. If it got back to the Navy that they were married and had a kid. They would most likely be in some hot water and ,for sure, wouldn't be allowed to work together. "Hey." He said in a low voice as she walked out. "Hey." She said back. "Have you talked to your mother? How's

Mitchelle?" He moved a little closer. "Yes, I talked to her last night. She is doing good." Jessica looks over at him. "As much as I want to be here with you. I can't wait for my enlistment to be done so I can get home to her." He reaches out and grabs her hand. "I know it won't belong." She shakes her head. "I got to get back. I will see you on the copter." She turns and walks back inside. He waits for a moment and then follows her back inside and back down to his men and finishes getting ready.

About 10 minutes later, Slone and his Alfa team walked toward and started boarding their helicopter. Slone looked over at the pilot and winked at Jessica as he walked to his seat.

For the next hour, they flew in mostly silence. There was not much to say. They all knew what they had to do. They just needed to keep going over it in their minds.

He heard Jessica's voice come over the com system. "We will be over the drop zone in 5 minutes." Slone then pulled up the satellite image of the compound. He looked over at his men. "We have heat signatures of 10 hostiles. One of them is Omar Alead. OK, let's do our job, Men!"

They all got up and moved into position. When they felt the copter stop and hover. Slone shouted. "Go!" They dropped 4 ropes from both sides of the copter and each man grabbed a rope and slid down it to the ground. Bravo team did the same thing on the backside of the compound.

On the ground, they ran for the door. When they got ther,e they broke the door down with a battering ram and entered the compound. They fanned out 4 men on each side and cleared out the front room. They then entered the main room from the front as Bravo team entered from the back. They saw the 10 hostiles on their knees. They spread out around the room with guns trained on them. The hostiles were not making any moves. They were praying. Slone quickly looked around the room and saw C4 explosives on the walls all around them. It was a trap. Slone yelled. "Abort! Get out of here!"

There was no time to get out the way they came. Slone turned and started running toward a large window. When he got there, he lunged into in with his gun out in front of him. The window shattered as he went through, as he heard the explosion go off behind him. The force of the blast propelled him forward. He hit the ground hard. Knocking the wind out of him. He lay there on the ground for a moment. His head was spinning. He rolled over and threw the fire and smoke. He saw a man standing at the edge of the woods. He made eye contact with the man. It was O'mar Alead. He felt for his rifle, but it had lost it in the blast. He felt for his sidearm. But it was also missing. Alead then turned and ran into the woods.

He tried to get up. Then, the pain hit him. His knee was hurt, and he was bleeding from several cuts from flying glass. He could feel the blood running down his face. He reached for his radio. He started to call for help. But if he broke radio silence, the enemy would know he was alive. He would be a sitting duck. He put it down. Charlie team would be here soon.

He could hear a helicopter. He looked around. He saw it. It looked like Jessica's copter. She must have heard his call to abort and was returning. He felt for his flare gun. But it was also gone. He needed to find a way to signal her. About that time,, he saw what he recognized as a heat-seeking missile headed toward her helicopter. "No!" He shouted at the missile hit the helicopter. It started spinning hard and exploded and fell to the ground. He got on his knees and desperately tried to crawl in that direction. But he was overcome with pain and fell back. No, this could not be happening! He tried again to get up. But again fell back in pain. He rolled over on his back and slowly slipped into unconsciousness.

*

(Present day)

Slone stood up. He looked back over at Jessica's headstone. The roses looked nice. He stepped over, kissed his fingers, and placed them on her name. Rest in peace, baby.

He took a few steps away, then turned and looked back at the two headstones. That's the day he started on the path to where he is today. That's the day his life changed forever!

Chapter 5

Carter buttoned up this Sheriff's Department shirt and tucked it in as he looked in the mirror. He hoped today went better. He had not slept well. Although he didn't remember the last time he did. Things seem to just be getting worse at work. But today was the day he was going to start turning that around. He was driving to Huntsville to talk to Mike McKinney. So somehow. Some way he was going to convince him, to tell him what all he knew about his father's business. He knew Doyle McKinney was behind the killings. The one thing all the victims had in common was that they had a connection to Mike's trial. Judge, District Attorney, Jury members. Then something happened, and the killer turned on Doyle McKinney and killed him. Then everything stops. Mike McKenney knew something, and he was going to find out what it was.

He turned and walked out of the bathroom. He grabbed his gun holster and put it on. He then opened his gun safe, took out His Papaw's 38, checked the load, and put it in his holster.

He turns and walks into the living room and meets Carolyn and Becky. Carolyn walks by and says. "I will be late again tonight. I'm trying to see if I can get something going." She stops and turns around. "We are headed to the car. Will you please tell Tom to come on." Carter turns to look at her. "Y'all go on. I will take Tom. Something I need to talk to him about."

Carolyn turns toward the door. "Fine. Come on, Becky." Becky walks toward him. She smiles and hugs him. "Bye, Daddy. Have a good day." She kisses him on the cheek. He smiles and says. "You too, sweetheart."

He watches them walk out the door. He smiles. No matter how bad things get. Becky always makes him feel better.

He turns and walks toward Tom's room. When he gets to the door, he hears a thud. He wonders what that is. Slowly opening the door, he sees a piece of plywood hanging up and something sticking into it. He turns and looks at Tom, who has another one of the objects in his hand. "What are you doing?" Tom looks at him and smiles. "I'm throwing ninja stars." He holds one up for his Dad to see. It's star-shaped with very sharp edges. Tom then threw it at the plywood. It hits in the center. Carter looks at him. "Where did you get those?" Tom turns. "I bought them from a friend. Are they cool or what?" Carter looks at him with a stern look on his face. "What friend?" Tom turns and faces his Dad and puts his hands up. "Wo Dad. I think I need a lawyer!" Carter walks over and pulls one out of the plywood. "These are sharp!" Tom looks at him and says. "Well ya, Dad, that's kinda the point. You really don't want dull ninja stars." Carter holds one up and says. "You could hurt yourself with these or worse yet. You could put a hole in your Mom's wall. That could get you killed." Tom smiles. "I'm good at it, Dad. Not going to do that." Carter lays the star down. "Well, at least take it outside." Tom shakes his head. "Ok, Dad, if that makes you feel better."

Carter looks over at Tom with a serious look on his face and says. "Hey, Tom, there is something I want to talk to you about. Have you heard what happened with Steven Smith yesterday?" Tom looks back at his Dad. "Ya, I heard. Is Steven going to be ok?" Carter nods his head. "Ya, he is going to be ok. I'm going to make sure that he gets the help he needs. But what he really needs is friends his own age to whom he can talk. Somebody he can confide in, to get things off his chest if he needs to. I guess what I'm asking, son, is if you can reach out to this kid and befriend him. It could make a huge difference."

Tom shakes his head. "Sure, Dad. Steven and I are friends. I knew he was having a hard time after his mother died. I guess I should have been a better friend, to begin with." Carter puts his arm around Tom. "Well, son, you can't always know what is going on in somebody's head.

You just have to be there for them as best you can." Tom looks up at him. "Will do Dad."

Carter turns for the door. "Let's get out of here, or we are going to be late." They walk through the house. Carter grabs his cowboy hat off the rack as they go out the door.

They make the short drive to the Groesbeck High School. Carter pulls up in front. He looks out and sees two girls waving at Tom. Tom turns to his Dad and says. "What can I say, Dad. When you got it, you got it." Carter smiles. "Have a good day, son." Tom looks over at him. "Later Dad." He then jumps out.

Carter then makes the drive over to the Sheriff's Department. Walking inside, he speaks to several people on his way to his office. He sees Deputies Roberts and Hayes and motions for them to join him in his office.

He enters and sits down at his desk. Roberts and Hayes join him. They sat down in the chair across from the desk. At about that time, Nancy walks in carrying a pot of coffee. She hands Roberts and Hayes a cup and pours them some coffee. She then picks up the cup on Carter's desk and pours him some. She then smiles. "That should fix y'all up." She then walks out.

The three men look at each other. Carter stands up and walks over to the potted plant in the corner of the office and pours his coffee out. Roberts and Hayes each do the same thing. Hayes looks over at Carter. "You know you're going to kill that plant someday." Carter sits back down at his desk. "Ya, I know. But it's the only reason it's here. When it dies, I'll get Nancy to get me another one."

Roberts and Hayes sit down. Carter looks at them. "I'm going to take a drive over to Huntsville today. I'm going to talk to Mike McKinney. I'm going to rattle his cage and get him to tell me what he knows about his Dad, Doyle McKinney, and his dealings with our Killer." Roberts then says. "What makes you think he will help us?" "Well," Carter says. "What's he got to lose? His Dad is dead now. He is rotting in jail. I think it's worth a shot. Not like we got a lot to go on." Roberts and Hayes nod their heads yes.

Carter stands up. "Can you hold down the fort while I'm gone?" "Sure, boss," Roberts says, standing up. Carter walks around them to the door. "Good. I will call you and let you know what I find out. I will be back as quick as I can."

Carter walks through the bull pin toward the door. He stops at Nancy's desk. "I will be out of the office awhile. Call if you need me." She looks at him and smiles. "Will Do, Sheriff."

Carter got in his car and headed toward Huntsville, Texas. He made the 80-plus-mile trip in a little over an hour.

He entered the prison and went through security, checking his weapon. He asks to see Mike McKenney. He was sent to the interview area and waited for almost an hour. The door opens, and a guard brings McKenney in. McKenney sits down across from Carter. The guard looks at Carter and says. "Do you need anything, Sheriff?" Carter looks up. "No, thank you." The guard nods. "Knock on the door when you're done." "Thank you," Carter says. The guard then leaves, closing the door behind him.

There is a moment of awkward silence as the two men look at each other. McKenney then says. "Well, you're the one person I never expected to see here. So what do I owe the pleasure Sheriff? My rec is coming up, and I would really hate to miss my one chance a day to get out of that cell you put me in. So let's cut to the chase, Sheriff. What's this about?" Carter looks over at him. "I'm investigating your father's murder. There are some things I think you can help me with." McKenney smiles big. "Even if I could help you. Why would you ever think I would?" Carter looks across the table. "Because you were sentenced to 20 years in here. You're going to do at least 10. You have served about 2. Do you really want to do another 8 years here? Or do you help me, and I see what I can do to help you?" McKenney sat in silence and looked at Carter. Carter shook his head. "All your father's money is just sitting in a bank, and you can't touch it. So what's it going to be?" McKenney looks away, then back to Carter. "Ok, I help you, and you get me out of here! I have your word on that?" Carter looks at him and says. "I told you I will do what I can. That's the best I can do. You have my word on that." McKenney nods. "What do you want to know?"

Carter then says. "OK, first let me tell you what I already know. I know your father hired a man to kill the persons connected to your trial and conviction. I also know that man later turned on your father and killed him. I need to know. Who this man is? And anything you know that might help me find him?"

There was silence for a moment. McKenney then said. "First, I don't know who the man is. But I do know that my father had connections. So finding a man like that would not be a problem." "What kind of connections?" Carter asked. "The same kind of connections that landed me in here." Carter gave him a confused look. "Ok, you're going to have to explain that. Start at the beginning."

McKenney looked over at Carter. "Ok. Several years ago. My father was approached by a man from some part of the Government. I think his name was Hunter. He was trying to raise money to fight the Taliban and, later, ISIS in Afghanistan. But Congress was blocking sending money directly. So it had to be an under-the-table thing, with no paper trail back to us. So we set up this drug operation. We got a cut. But most of the money went to the Afghanistan slush fund that Hunter ran."

"They told us we would be protected from the cops." Carter smiled at him. "Well, they told you wrong." McKenney holds his hands up and looks around. "Apparently so!" Carter then says. "Ok, what I don't get. Your father was a rich man. Why would he risk this? For just a cut of the money?" McKenney looked over at Carter. "Power. My father was a big fish in a small pond. He wanted to be a bigger fish in a bigger pond. I think he was promised ambassadorship somewhere. My father's lust for power made it impossible for him to turn it down."

McKenney then looks at Carter and frowns. "We had a smooth operation going on. We were fighting terrorism, making a little money. Then you had to go and stick your nose in it and fuck the whole thing up. You had to have somebody undercover. I just don't know who it was. I knew every cop and deputy in Limestone County."

"OK," Carter says. "You get busted. Found guilty, Sentenced. What sends your father over the edge?" "Well," McKenney says, "He felt betrayed. We didn't get any help from the people we were trying to help. It was like they just cut bait and moved on and let me take the fall. He was really upset about that. His son was in jail. There was nothing leading back to him. But his reputation was damaged."

Carter then says. "So your dad then goes off the deep end and hires a hitman to kill everybody that had anything to do with your trial? McKenney shakes his head. "Yes." Carter looks back at him. "But you got no idea who he hired or why he turned on him and killed him?" "No," McKenney said. "But my father kept all his important papers and stuff in the safe out at our cabin at Old Union." McKenney takes a piece of paper and writes down the address and combination of the safe. There is a key above the door."

Carter takes the paper. "I have your permission to search the cabin?" McKenney shakes his head. "Yes", Carter stands up. "I will keep my word. I will talk to the judge. Do what I can."

The guard comes in and leads McKenney out. He turns. "Thank you, Sheriff."

Carter made his way out of prison. He called Roberts and told him what he had found out. He asked him and Hayes to meet him at the Old Union address and call a judge to get a search warrant. McKenney had given him permission to search, but it would be better with a warrant just in case.

He got to the cabin first and waited at the gate for them to arrive. He got out and looked around. He could see the cabin about 75 yards from the gate. The gate was locked, and it didn't look like anybody had been here.

Roberts and Hayes pulled up and got out. Carter said, "You get it?" Roberts held a piece of paper up and said, "Got it." Hayes pulled out a pair of bolt cutters from the car, cut the lock off the gate, and swung the gate open. They both got back in their cars and drove down to the cabin.

Parking in front, they got out and walked up to the door. Carter knocked. He really didn't expect anybody to be home, but he knocked anyway after a few moments. Carter says. "Ok, nobody's home." He then taped a copy of the warrant to the door. Hayes then moves to the center of the door and lifts his foot to kick the door. "Look out, I got this." Carter held out his hand to stop him. "Hang on." Carter then reaches up above the door and grabs the key. He looks over at Hayes. "Why don't we try this first?" Carter unlocks the door, looks over at Hayes, and shrugs. Hayes looks back. "I guess that will work. I could have kicked it in one try. Would have busted right open." Carter and Roberts look at each other and back at Hayes. "Oh ya, we know", Carter says.

Carter then pushes open the door, and they walk in. They look around. The cabin is really nice for a hunting cabin. But he didn't think much hunting went on here. They walked into a large living room. Quickly looking around, Carter found the room that must have been Doyle McKenney's office. Entering, he looked around. He called out to Roberts and Hayes. "Hey, in here." They joined him in the office. "There is a safe in here someplace." Carter walks behind the desk and sees it. "Here it is." He says.

Carter takes the paper out of his pocket, sits down in the desk chair, and moves over to the safe. He looks at the numbers on the paper and works the lock. He grabs the handle and turns it. The safe pops open.

There are four thick files in it. He takes them out and puts them on the desk. He looks through them. 2 of them are just some business files. 1 of them is on the drug operation. Then he opened the last file. It was smaller than the others. It looked like military files on soldiers. The first two were men that Carter did not know. But when he looked at the Picture in the 3rd file. He stared at it for a long moment. "What is it, John?" Roberts asks. Carter looked up. "This is him." He said. "This is our guy. Lieutenant Commander Jake Slone." Carter smiled as he looked through the file. A lot of it had been blacked out. "It says here he was a Decorated Navy Seal. He has a Silver Star and two Bronze Stars for valor under fire. Two purple hearts." Carter looks up at them. "He's a war hero!"

Roberts shakes his head. "That can't be right. How do you go from war hero to cold-blooded killer?" Carter flips through some more pages. "Well, I can do you one better than that. Says here he was killed in action little over 10 years ago."

They all look at each other. Cater says. "We are looking for a dead man!"

Chapter 6

Slone walked back out the front gate of the cemetery. He briefly looked around to see if anyone was around. He seemed to do this out of habit. But it was a good habit to have.

He got in his truck and started it up. He looked at the clock. It was 12:15 pm. He needed to head for his meeting spot with his contact, Nathan Hunter.

He made the drive down the famous U.S Route 66. Several miles down the road, he pulled into a large parking lot and parked the truck. Looking up at the name on the building. H.A. Chapman Stadium. Home of the Golden Hurricane. He got out and walked toward the stadium. It was on the campus of the University of Tulsa. He had briefly gone to school here right before joining the Navy. He had enjoyed his time here. He often wondered what would have happened if he had stayed here in school.

The football team was practicing, so the stadium was open to the public. He stopped briefly and looked at the bronze statue of Glenn Dobbs right outside the front gate.

When he got inside, he looked over at the field. It was a nice artificial turf. They had done some work on the stadium since he had been here. There was a large end zone scoreboard. On the other end, they had taken out the bleachers and built the Case Athletic Complex. It looks like they added some box seats. But it could probably only seat about 30,000 people. It was very small by college football standards.

He climbed up about halfway on the 50-yard line and sat down. A few players had started coming out. He was a few minutes early. He knew that Hunter would scout the place out before he showed himself. So he waited.

He had known Nathan Hunter for over 10 years now. He didn't know if Nathan Hunter was even his real name. But it didn't matter. He was the closest thing to a friend he had. He had helped him through some very hard times back in Afghanistan. He had stood by him through all the mess of the last year. He owed him his life several times over.

*

(Afghanistan 10 years earlier)

Lieutenant Commander Jake Slone slowly opened his eyes. His eyesight came into focus. His left eye was swollen almost shut. He looked around. He was in a small room. He moved and felt pain in his lower body. He looked to his left and saw an IV in his left arm. His right knee was bandaged. He tried to set up but fell back in pain.

A moment later, he heard someone come walking in the door. His eyes focused on the man, and he could see it was Sergeant Jim Dorsey, his friend from back home, they had joined the Navy together. Dorsey smiled as he walked to the bed. "You're awake, buddy. I was really worried about you. How are you feeling?" Slone slowly looked up at Dorsey. "What happened? Where am I?" Dorsey's smile disappeared as he looked down on his friend. "We were on a raid. We were after O'mar Alead. We were ambushed."

Slone stared at Dorsey as the memories came back. He remembered dropping out of the helicopter, busting the door down, and making his way inside. He saw the men praying and then the C-4 on the wall. His call to abort. Running through the window. The explosion. Seeing O'mar Alead running away. Then the last memory. The helicopter getting hit by the missile.

He looked up at Dorsey with a look of desperation in his eyes. "Was it her helicopter? Did she get out?" A sad look came over Dorsey's face as he looked down on his hurt friend. "It was Jessica's Helicopter and she didn't make it."

Slone lowered his head and put his hand in his face, hoping to somehow hold back the tears. Dorsey put his hand on his shoulder and quietly watched as his friend sobbed for a few moments. He was one of the few who knew about him and Jessica, so he understood just how hard this hit him.

Slone looked up at Dorsey. "They knew we were coming! We walked right into it!" Dorsey shook his head. "Ya, I know. There is an investigation going on. There have been some people coming around asking questions. Charlie team, and you are all that's left. We are grounded until the investigation is done."

There was a long moment of silence, and then Slone said. "We are going to get this guy. Alead is going to pay for what he has done!" Dorsey shook his head. "Damn right we are going to get that son of a bitch!"

Dorsey stood up. "Hey, I gotta go. I'm not really supposed to be here. But I had to make sure you were doing ok. Hang in there. I'm here for you if you need me." Slone held up his hand, and Dorsey took it. "Thank you." Dorsey forced a small smile. "I will check back when I can." Slone nodded, and Dorsey turned and left.

Slone laid his head back. A few tears ran down his face. He reached for the pain button on his IV. He punched it several times. A few minutes later, he fell asleep.

He awoke to a loud knock on the door. He looked up to see two men standing in the doorway. One was in civilian clothes and the other was dressed in a Navy Captain's uniform. The Captain looked over at him. "Lieutenant Commander Slone?" The man said. Slone nodded his head and said. "Yes, Sir." The two men took a few steps toward his bed. The Captain said. "I'm Captain Lewis with the Office of Naval Intelligence, This is N.C.I.S. Agent Dunn. We have some questions for you, Commander." Slone looked up at them and said. "Yes, sir. Anything I can do to help."

Captain Lewis pulled a tape recorder out of his pocket and pushed record. Agent Dunn then pulled out his notepad, looked at Slone, and said. "Ok, before the raid. Did you notice anything out of the ordinary?" "No," Slone said. Everything went just as planned. Just like every other raid I have been a part of." Dunn then asked. "When did you first notice that things were going bad? Slone paused for a moment and then said. "When we entered the compound, we didn't encounter any resistance. When we got to the center room, I saw several combatants on their knees praying. I looked around, saw the C-4 on the walls, and realized what was happening. I called for an abort, saw a window, and ran for it and jumped through it as the C-4 went off. I was thrown clear of the building and landed hard on the ground. I looked around and saw mission target O'mar Alead running away."

Captain Lewis and Agent Dunn looked at each other and then back at Slone. Capital Lewis then spoke. "How is it that you were the only survivor?" Slone then thought for a moment, then said. "I was the first and maybe the only person to see the C-4, and I was reacting first. I called for the abort and ran toward the window, expecting them to follow me. There was not much time." Agent Dunn then said. "So you chose to save yourself?" Slone looked over at Dunn with a frown on his face. "No, it was not like that. They just didn't have time to make it."

Lewis and Dunn looked at each other again. Then Captain Lewis said. "Commander. How many men were on Alpha and Bravo teams?" Slone then looked up and said. "There were two eight-man teams. So there were 16 of us." Lewis then looked down on Slone and said. "Ok then, if you are the only survivor and the rest were killed. We should have recovered 15 bodies, is that correct, Commander?" Slone, with a confused look on his face, said. "Yes, sir." Agent Dunn then said. "OK, explain how we have 16 bodies?" Slone frowned and said. "I don't know. There were combatants who were praying. There were more than just us in the room." Dunn nodded. "That's what we thought at first. But then we separated them out. We have 16 bodies and 16 dog tags. So we did some looking at the names on those tags. Guess what? Lewis then hands Slone a picture of a set of dog tags. Slone looks at it in disbelief. Captain Lewis then says. "Ya, that's right. The tags in that picture say. Lieutenant Commander Jake Slone. So, explain how your tags got on that body? Or better yet. How are they still around your neck? "Slone shakes his head. I don't know. There must be some kind of mistake!" Agent Dunn then smiles. "Oh, it doesn't end there, Commander. That same body. Was dressed in this." He pulls out another picture and shows it to Slone. The picture shows a desert camo uniform shirt with the name Slone over the pocket. Slone looks at it in shock. Then the Captain says. "Oh, we saved the best for last." He pulls out a piece of paper and hands it to Slone. "That's your bank account." He then points to a place on the paper. "This is a deposit in the amount of 10,000 dollars made the day before the raid! Care to explain that, Commander?" Slone looks up and says. "I have no idea where that money came from! You've got to believe me! I don't know anything about any of this!"

There was a long moment of silence. Then Agen Dunn says. "Ok, Commander. Let us tell you what we know, then. You sold out! You sold out your men. You sold out your country! You made a deal with Alead for info on the raid. That's what the 10,000 dollars is for. You planned to get out before the bomb went off. They had an extra body planted to look like you died in the raid. But you didn't get out in time, and your buddy Alead left you.

That's what we think happened. You're going to be charged with everything from aiding the enemy. To conspiracy to commit murder to murder, and last but not least, treason! You're going to spend the rest of your life in prison.

Slone felt sick inside. He didn't know what to do. He slowly raised his head and looked at the two men standing by his bed. "I think I'm going to need a lawyer."

The two men took a step back away from the bed. Captain Louis then said. "Ok, Commander. We will send a lawyer over with a copy of the charges. Your best hope is that he is a good one. Your damn sure going to need one!"

The two men turned and walked out. Slone laid his head back. This could not be happening! It just couldn't get any worse than this. What was he going to do!

A few hours later. Slone heard a knock on the door. He looked up to see a tall, dark-haired man in civilian clothes standing in the doorway. The man looked at Slone and said. "Lieutenant Commander Slone?" Slone nodded his head. "Yes, sir." Slone didn't feel much like talking. What could this guy want?

The man walked up closer to the bed and took out his ID. "I'm Nathan Hunter with the Central Intelligence Agency. If you feel up to it. I would like to have a word with you." Slone lowered his head. Great. Now the C.I.A. was coming after him. He looked up and met the man's eyes. "Sir. Like I told the investigators. I didn't have anything to do with what happened on that raid. I'm not saying anything else till I have talked to a lawyer.

Hunter put his ID away and took a step closer. "Well, Commander. I believe you, and that's not why I'm here." Slone looked at him with a confused look on his face. "Then why are you here?" Hunter smiled at him. "I'm here to help you. I have looked at your file. Decorated war hero. Not the type of person to sell out his country. But whoever set you up. Did a good job. You're looking at best, spending the rest of your life in prison. While this terrorist O'mar Alead. The man who killed your men is still out there. I can help you. I can make all of this go away. Come work with me and we can find Alead and bring him to justice."

Slone looked up at him. Not sure if he was believing what he was hearing. Was this guy offering him a job? "What about the Navy? How can you make this go away?"

Hunter pulls up a chair and sits down. You're scheduled for surgery in the morning to remove some shrapnel from your abdomen, as far as the world will know. You will die of complications of wounds you receive in a raid. The investigation will end with your death. You will be buried as a war hero, and your family will be very well taken care of by the Navy and the CIA. Then you can continue to serve your country. Or you can spend the rest of your life in prison. No help for your family. It's your choice, Commander. But I need to know before you go into surgery in the morning.

Hunter reaches into his pocket, pulls out a cheap cell phone, and hands it to Slone. "There is one number programmed into this phone. If you're interested, give me a call. But don't wait too long." Hunter turns and walks out, leaving Slone speechless.

*

(Present Day)

Slone sat and watched the players come out and start practice. He could feel Nathan Hunter approaching, even though he heard nothing. Then a voice from behind him said, "Hello, Jake. Have you been waiting long?" Slone turned his head, now seeing Hunter approaching him from the left. You know exactly how long I have been waiting, unless you have lost your edge. You were here before I was."

Hunter smiled and sat down. He looks out on the field and watched the team run a play. "So tell me. What the fuck is a Golden Hurricane?" Slone slowly turned his head and looked at him. "It's the mascot." Hunter smiled. "Well ya! But what the fuck is it? I never heard of a Golden Hurricane. You went to school here, I thought you would know." Slone laffed. "I was here for one semester before the Navy. The University of Miami had already taken the name Hurricanes. I guess they were trying to be different." Hunter looked across the field. 'Well, they got different alright."

Hunter then handed Slone a brown envelope. Slone opened it up and took out the contents. On top was a picture of a man in a Captain's Navy uniform. Hunter then said. "This is Captain Marvin Briggs. He was an up-and-coming officer in the Navy till about 5 years ago. The wife and kids left him. Developed a drinking problem. His career went down the toilet. The last straw came at a party in Washington. He got drunk and did a lot of talking with reporters present. He was very critical of the president and his policies. It wound up on the news and every paper in the country. The President didn't take kindly to it. He forced Captain Briggs into retirement. He transferred him to the Naval Air Station in Dallas till his commitment is up in a few months. Briggs was very upset about this. The Navy was all he had left. He was targeted by the Russians. They have been grooming him for months. Befriending him in bars. We think he is fixing to sell classified info to them. We think this is going to go down next week at his Ellis County, Texas, ranch. Just south of Waxahachie, Texas. Your assignment is to eliminate Captain Briggs and any Russian agents and recover the information. Make Briggs look like suicide. Dispose of the others."

Slone was silent momentarily while he looked through the file on Briggs. He looks over at Hunter. "So when Briggs leaves with the info. Why don't you just arrest him?" Hunter looks back over at Slone. "It's not that simple. We arrest him. It hits the news. We have a public trial. Press will have a field day. Everybody will look bad. We will have an international incident with the Russians. This way, it's over quickly and quietly. Distraught Captain kills himself. End of story." Slone nods. "Ok, I get that. But what about the Russians? They are going to be pissed that we killed their agents?" Hunter smiles. "Sure, they will. But what can they say or do about it? Without admitting they were spying. Plus, we will be sending a strong message that this will not be tolerated." "Ok," Slone said. "I'm on it."

The two men sat and watched a few plays down on the field. Hunter then said. "How's Mitchelle doing?" Slone paused for a moment. "She is not doing very well. She is getting weaker by the day. Her doctors say she needs a heart transplant. She is on the list. But who knows if one will be available in time. Hunter puts his hand on Slone's shoulder as he stands up. "I'm really sorry to hear that, Jake. I know some people. I will make some calls and see if I can help." Slone looks up. "Thank you, Nathan. I know I can always count on you." Hunter pats Slone on the shoulder. "Hang in there." As he turns and walks away.

Slone sits there for a moment thinking of Mitchelle. Then he looks down at the file. He had to put Mitchelle out of his mind right now. He had to focus. He looked at the picture of Captain Marvin Briggs. Trader Sold out his country. He was going to enjoy putting a bullet in him!

Chapter 7

John Carter sat at his desk. Drinking his 2nd cup of Nancy's really bad coffee. He was looking through the files he found in Doyle McKinney's cabin. He had already called the Navy after spending almost an hour on hold. He had talked to a clerk there. All he could tell him was that Lieutenant Commander Jake Slone had died in Afghanistan 10 years ago. He told them he was alive and in Groesbeck a few months ago. They said that was impossible. So basically a waste of time.

Deputy Greg Roberts walks into the office. "Well, Sheriff. While you were on the phone with the Navy. I made some calls. Found a death certificate for Jake Slone in Tulsa, Oklahoma. His next of kin is listed as his mother. Still showing to live in Tulsa."

Carter looked over at him. "You have an address on the Mother?" Roberts looked down at his papers. "Yes, Maggy Slone, Tulsa, Oklahoma." "Well," Carter said. "Looks like I'm going to Tulsa."

Roberts hands him the papers and says. "I'll go with you." Carter stands up. "No. I may be gone for a few days. I need you here." Roberts then says. "Well, at least take Hayes with you." Carter thinks for a moment. "No, I'm sure it will just be an interview."

Carter then gathers up a few things, calls Carolyn, and tells her he will be gone. She seems not to care. They had both been under a lot of stress. A Little time apart would probably do them both some good. He runs by the house, gathers up a few things, and heads out on the six-hour trip to Tulsa, Oklahoma.

Carter made good time, making it in 5 ½ hours. But it was after 5 p.m., and he was sure the local Sheriff had gone home. He wanted to check in as a courtesy before going to see Maggie Slone. He decided to check into a hotel for the night. He was tired and ready for a break.

He pulled into the Red Roof Inn, the first motel he saw after he decided to get one. It was nice enough for his needs, just a room with a bed, a shower, and maybe a little bit of air that was all he needed. He checked in and made it to his room.

Throwing his bag on the bed, he took out his laptop computer. He looked up the Tulsa County Sheriff's Office. It looked like the Sheriff's name was Jim Dorsey. It looked like he had been Sheriff for about four years. His bio said he was a Deputy before that and spent several years in the Navy. He would get with him in the morning. Now, he was going to get something to eat and hit the sack.

The next morning, Carter got up early, showered, and got dressed. He dressed in plain clothes as he always did when he was off duty or working out of County. Putting on his Silverbelly cowboy hat, he went down to the lobby for breakfast. He ate and drank a decent cup of coffee. He looked up the address for the Tulsa County Sheriff's Office. It was located at 303 W. 1st Street. That shouldn't be hard to find. He wanted to be there early before Sheriff Dorsey got busy. He got in the car, drove over, and arrived just after 9 am.

It was in a plain-looking building but much bigger than his office. Once inside, he asked to speak to the Sheriff's secretary, who directed him to her desk.

He walked up to her, and she looked up at him and smiled. "Yes, sir. Can I help you?" Carter smiled back at her. He pulled his badge out of his pocket and showed it to her. "I'm Sheriff John Carter from Limestone County, Texas. If Sheriff Dorsey has a moment, I would like to have a brief word with him." She stood up and said. "Is Sheriff Dorsey expecting you?" "No," Carter said. She walked around her desk. "If you will just have a seat. Help yourself to some coffee." She walked around the corner.

Carter walked over and poured himself a cup of coffee. He took one sip and knew, "Wow, this was good coffee." He looked at the coffee maker. It looked just like his. So now he knew. Good coffee could be made with the equipment he had.

She came back around the corner and said to him. Right, this way, Sheriff. He followed her to a door. She opened the door for him, and he walked in. She left and closed the door behind her. The man behind the desk stood up, came around his desk, and offered his hand. "I'm Sheriff Jim Dorsey. What can I do for you?" Carter shook his hand and said. " I'm Limestone County, Texas Sheriff John Carter." Dorsey smiled. "Please have a seat." Carter sits down, and Dorsey returns to the seat behind his desk.

Carter then begins. "About 6 months ago, my county and surrounding areas had a string of murders. We came close to catching him. But he got away. To make a long story short. Recently, we found new evidence to ID our suspect. We believe he is from here in Tulsa. I would like to interview his mother. I'm here as a courtesy. Just to let you know I'm in town and what I'm doing."

Dorsey nods his head. "Thank you for keeping me in the loop. Would you like me to send a deputy with you?" Carter shook his head. "No, that won't be necessary. It's just an interview. May lead nowhere." Dorsey then said. "What's the mother's name?" Carter takes a sip of his coffee. "Maggie Slone."

Dorsey looks up with a surprised look on his face. "Maggie Slone?" He asks. "Yes," Carter says. Dorsey then stares at Carter and says. "The suspect, would that be Jake Slone?" Now it was Carter's turn to give a surprised look. "You know them?" Dorsey sits back in his chair. "Yes, I do. Jake was my best friend in High School. We joined the Navy together. I was on his Navy SEAL team in Afghanistan. I wish you had called before you made this trip out here. I could have saved you some time. Jake Slone was killed in Afghanistan about 10 years ago."

Carter paused for a moment. Caught off guard by what Dorsey had just told him. Then he said. "Are you sure he died. I have a positive ID off his Navy picture. That was found in the person who hired him's files." Dorsey took a hard look at him. "Yes, I'm sure! I was there on the raid. I'm the one who found him barely alive. He died a few days later during surgery. Your witness must be mistaken."

"Well," Carter said. "I guess I should have called first." Carter stands up, as does Dorsey. The two men shake hands. Dorsey then says. "I'm sorry, Sheriff. Have a safe trip back to Texas." "Thank you," Carter says as he turns to walk out. Dorsey looks after him and says. "Oh, Sheriff. Please don't bother Ms. Slone. The poor woman has been through a lot. Carter nods his head as he walks out the door.

Carter walks outside to his car. He gets in and sits there for a minute, wondering what just happened. He doesn't see any reason to antagonize the Sheriff if he and Slone were friends. So he sees no reason to tell him that the witness is him.

But he didn't drive all this way just to go home now. He pulled out the directions to Maggie Slone's home. It would take him about 20 minutes to get there. He used those 20 minutes to think about what he was going to say to her.

When he pulled up and parked in front of the house, he looked around. It was a nice small house. There was a red mid-size car parked in the driveway. As he got out and walked to the door, he didn't see anything out of the ordinary. There was a birdbath in the yard with a statue in it.

Getting to the door, he knocked. A few moments later, the door slowly opened to show an older lady with silver hair. She smiled. "Can I help you?" She said. Carter returned the smile. He pulled out his badge and showed it to her. "I'm Sheriff John Carter From Limestone County, Texas. Are you Maggie Slone?" The woman nods her head. "Yes, Sir." She said. Carter then says. "I would like to have a few words with you about an important matter. If you have time?" She hesitated for a moment. He could see a little bit of fear in her eyes. She then said. "Yes, of course, come in."

They walked down a short hall to what looked like a living room. There was a young girl sleeping on the couch, wrapped up in a blanket. The TV was on, but nobody was watching. They walked on through to a dining area in the kitchen. She pulled out a chair and sat down. "Please have a seat, Sheriff. Can I get you some coffee?" Carter smiled as he sat down. "No, thank you. I'm good."

As they both sat down. She looks over at him. "How can I help your Sheriff?" Carter looks over at her. "Ms. Slone, it's about your son. Jake Slone. I understand that he was in the Navy and was killed in action some time ago. But I have reason to believe he is alive. Have you had any contact with him?" She then looked toward the living room and then back at him. "There must be some kind of mistake. My son was killed in Afghanistan about 10 years ago. He wanted nothing else but to serve his country. He enlisted the year after he graduated from High School. He won several medals for bravery. I can assure you he has passed on to a better place."

Carter nodded. "Is that offer for coffee still good?" She smiled and stood up. "Yes, of course." She walked into the kitchen. He really didn't want the coffee. He just needed a moment to regroup. He saw some pill bottles sitting on the table. He quickly reached over, picked the bottles up, and looked at them. They were for prescriptions for a Michelle Slone. They were Eplerenone and Spironolactone. He pulled out his phone and took a picture of the bottles. He had never heard of them. He would look it up later. He heard her coming back and quickly put the bottles back.

She handed him the coffee cup. He looked up at her. "Thank you." She sat back down and took a sip of her coffee. "Now, Sheriff. You have come a long way. What makes you think my son is alive?" Taking a sip of his own coffee, he puts it down and reaches into his sports coat pocket. He pulls out the dashcam picture taken by the Mart Police and shows it to her. She picks it up and looks at it. "Well, this picture is kinda fuzzy. It looks a little like my son. But it looks like a lot of people. You didn't come all this way just to show me that?" Carter smiled as he put the picture back in his pocket. He felt like he was the one being questioned now. He had caught her off guard initially, but she had regrouped and now was fishing for info. He took another sip of his coffee. Stalling for a moment, trying to think of where to go from there. Even if she knew he was alive. She was not going to give him up. Everything he told her could go straight back to Slone. He didn't want to put all his cards on the table.

He looked over at her. "Well, I'm just trying to tie up some loose ends. I guess if he is not my guy, I can move on. I had to check out every angle. I hope you understand." He takes one last sip of his coffee and stands up. "Thank you for your time, Ms. Slone." He shakes hands with her. She says. "You're welcome, Sheriff. Have a safe trip home." He smiles, "I will. Thank you."

He turns and walks toward the door with her behind him. Going back through the living room, the girl on the couch is awake and setting up, still wrapped in the blanket. She looks over at them and says, "Grandma, can you get me some water? I'm thirsty." Maggie looks over at her as they walk through. Yes, dear. I'll get it for you."

As Carter opens the door. Maggie says. "Sheriff, do you have a card you can leave?" Carter turns, surprised. "Yes, of course." He reaches into his billfold and pulls out one of his cards. And hands it to her. "Here you go. Have a great day."

Carter walks out, and she closes the door behind him. He walks down the driveway, stops, and looks back at the house. His gut was telling him that she knew more than what she was telling. The girl had called her Grandma. His records showed that Jake Slone was an only child. Was the child his? She would be about the right age. She looked sick. There were pills on the table. Was she Mitchelle? If her son was dead, and this was all a big mistake. Why did she ask for a card? Not adding up.

He walked down by her parked car. He reached in his pocket, pulled out a tracking device, and placed it under the back wheel well. He then walked to his car and got in. He drove around the block, came back, parked a block or so away, and watched. A few minutes later, Ms. Slone came out of the house, went out to the birdbath, and moved the statue in it to face the north. Now that was strange.

He checked the tracking device, and it was working. He would know if she moved. He got on the computer in the car. He looked up Memorial Park Cemetery. It was only a few miles away. Jake Slone was supposed to be buried there. I would not hurt to see what was out there.

So he started the car and made the drive over it was a bigger cemetery than he expected. He got out and walked into the building that housed the plot records. He looked up the name Jake Slone and got the plot number and its approx location.

Walking through the cemetery, he found the row number and started down it. He came across the headstone he was looking for, Jake Slone, with the birth and death dates that matched the ones he had. This had to be it. He pulled out his phone and took a picture of the headstone.

But what was interesting was the headstone next to his. The name on it was Jessica Slone. The death date was 3 days before Jake's. Both stones had a United States Navy seal on top of them. Could this be his wife? His Navy records showed him as single with no children. At the base of her stone. There were flowers. Fresh probably only a day or so old. Looking at the ground around the plot he could see a footprint and what looked like a knee imprint.

Somebody had nealed and placed flowers at her grave. The footprint was too big to be his mother's, and if it was her, she would have put the flowers on his grave, not hers.

He placed two five-dollar bills following the footprint. Each bill was 6 inches long, and they overlapped about 2 inches, so it was approximately a size 10 boot. He picked the bills up. It was a crude way to measure, but you made do with what you had. Standing up, he put the bills back in his wallet.

He knew it. He could feel it in his gut. He had been here! He stared at the headstone that said, Jake Slone. "I'm going to find you! I promise you that! If I got to look under every rock in Tulsa!"

Chapter 8

Leaving the Cemetery, Carter made his way back out to his car. Getting in. He sat behind the wheel for a moment. He needed to think. He could use some help. But after talking to Sheriff Dorsey. He didn't think he was going to get any there.

He pulled out his phone and called Deputy Roberts. It rang twice before Roberts picked up. "Morning, boss. How're things going up there?" Carter took a deep breath. "Oh, I don't know where to start," Carter said. "I get up here. Local Sheriff knows Slone. Went to school with him and was in the Navy together. He insists that he is dead. So no help there. Talk to the mom. She knows more than what she is telling. There is a 10-year-old kid that I think might be Slone's. Her name is Mitchelle Slone. I need you to check birth records from around 10 years ago. Mother's name may be Jessica Slone." Roberts then said. "Ok, I'm on it, boss, anything else?" "Ya," Carter says. "I need you to look up the drugs, Eplerenone, and Spironolactone. Find out what they are for. I think the kid might be sick." "Ok, got it," Roberts said. "Ok, good," Carter said. "Oh, and I think Slone is here in Tulsa somewhere. I will keep an eye on the Mom and see if she will lead me to him." "John, sounds like you've got your hands full up there. Let me send a few deputies up there to help you?" Roberts said. "No, Greg," Carter says. "Not yet anyway. Get that info for me, and we will go from there." "Will do," Roberts said. "Be Careful, John." "I will. Talk to you later."

Carter put his phone away and started the car. He drove back over to Maggie Slone's place and parked a few blocks away. He didn't want to park to close and take a chance of being seen. He could see the front of the house and the car with a small pair of binoculars. He sat and watched for a few hours. This was getting nowhere. There had been no movement. Somebody was going to take notice of his Limestone

County, Texas, patrol car sitting here. He decided to drive back to the motel. It was only a few miles away, and he had the tracker on the car. If she moved it, he would know.

He picked up something to eat and returned to the motel. Opening the door, he walked inside and set his food on the table. He didn't really feel like eating. He took his cowboy hat off and placed it by the nightstand and sat down on the bed.

About that time, his cell phone rang. He looked at the number. It was Roberts calling him back. He answered it. "Carter." He said. "Sheriff," Roberts said. "I think I got all that info you wanted." "Great. What did you find out?" Carter said. "I found out that those two drugs. Eplerenone and Spironolactone are used to treat heart problems. I also found a birth record for a Mitchelle Slone, a little over 10 years ago. Born to Mother Jessica Slone and Father Jake Slone." "Ok," Slone said. "So the girl is his daughter, and she has some kind of heart problems. Thanks, Greg. That's been a big help." "Sure, boss. How're things going?" "Nothing new yet," Carter said. "I'll keep you updated." "Ok, be careful, John," Roberts said, hanging up.

Carter put his phone away and checked the tracker. Nothing yet. He might as well eat. It looks like it could be a long night.

*

Slone packed his stuff in his travel trailer. He had stopped by the office and paid a few months in advance. He would head out to Dallas in the morning. He wanted to do some recon on Captain Briggs and know for sure when and where the exchange was going down.

He wanted to talk to his mom before he left and find out how Mitchelle was doing. He wanted to see her so badly.

He had everything packed. All he had to do was throw it in the truck in the morning. He started the truck and drove across town to where his mother lived. He was always cautious, driving by first and checking things out. He looked in the front yard and saw that the statue had been moved to face the north. That was their predetermined code, for there was some kind of problem.

Slone wondered what the problem could be. He sat there for several minutes. He wanted to go in and find out what was going on, but he resisted the urge.

He drove to the prearranged meeting place, a park near the house. He parked and waited. It was getting dark. She should be here soon.

*

Carter sat in his motel room. He had finished his dinner and was now just waiting. He had tried to watch some TV but couldn't get interested in anything. He had called and talked to Deputy Roberts again, and things were going okay at the office. He had called and talked to Carolyn. She seemed kind of distant, not much interested in talking. He was hoping a little time apart would help things between them. But so far, it didn't seem to be having that effect.

Didn't she see that he was trying to do everything he could to try to make things right and to fix his reputation? He just needed her to give him a little more time. This was the closest he had been. This might be the last chance to catch Slone and turn things around.

He looked out the window. It had been dark for about an hour. He lay down on the bed. He was just fixing to doze off to sleep when he heard the computer beep. Jumping up, now wide awake, he looked at his computer. Maggy Slone's car was on the move. He grabbed his gun shoulder holster and quickly put it on, then threw his sports coat over it. Grabbing his laptop computer, he ran out the door.

*

Slone saw the lights of his mother's car pull up in the park. He waited while she parked and walked up to the bench where they met at. He got out, looked around, and walked over to where she was.

"Hey, Mom, " he said as he walked around and sat down beside her. She smiled, grabbed, and squeezed his hand. "So what's up, Mom? " he said. She looked up at him and said, "I was contacted this morning by a Sheriff from Texas." She handed him the card. "He was asking questions about you?"

Slone looks at Carter's card and says. "What did you tell him?" She shakes her head. "I didn't tell him anything. I told him you were dead. Then he left."

Slone stands up. Carter would not have given up that easily. He looks around the park. He sees an outline of a man walking toward them with a cowboy hat and what looked like a gun in his hand. He can't get back to his truck without going past him. He looks down at his Mom. "Give me your car keys." She still has them in her hand. She hands them to him. Taking them from her, he gives his keys. "You were followed. I've got to go, Mom.

Slone starts running toward her car. He looks at the man running after him. He gets to her car, jumps in, and starts the engine. He backs out. He sees the man that he can now identify as Sheriff Carter coming up on the back of the car. He hears Carter yell, "Stop!" He puts the car in forward gear and takes off. Carter shoots twice at the car, breaking out the back window of the car.

Slone makes his way around the park. He sees Carter cutting across the grass to his patrol car. Slone turns to speed out of the park entrance. Carter is taking off behind him with lights flashing.

Slone hit the gas hard. He was building up speed. But his Mom's car was no match for Carter's car. He looked in his rearview mirror and could see Carter gaining on him. He weaved in and out and around cars in the two-lane southbound traffic. Carter had another advantage of his light. Cars saw the flashing light of his patrol car and got out of his way. So he was making up ground fast, till he was almost right behind him.

Slone had to think of something and fast. He was coming up on a traffic light. The light went from green to yellow. Slone pushed it hard through the yellow light. Barely making it there, he looked in his mirror to see what Carter would do.

Carter saw Slone go through the yellow light. He knew if he slowed down for the light, he would be gone. So he hit the gas to get through the now red light. Carter heard a horn and the bright light of a Mack truck to his left. He braced for impact as the heavy Mack truck hit him hard broadside. The car felt like it was airborne as it hit on its side and then rolled over on its top, and then back upright.

As it came to rest. The airbag had hit him in the face, as the bag deflated, his head was lying on the steering wheel. He tried to raise his head up, but fell back down and lost consciousness.

The next thing he knew, he heard the door open and felt some hands on him pulling him out of the car and onto the ground. He felt two fingers on his neck checking for a pulse. As he tried to open his eyes, he could see a blurry figure over him. As he tried to make his eyes focus, he could see that the man kneeling over him was Jake Slone.

He tried to reach for his gun, but Slone grabbed his arm. "No Sheriff, let's not do that," Slone said as he pulled Carter's gun out and slid it a few feet away. He looked down at Carter. "Just couldn't let it go, could ya?" Carter struggled to get up, but couldn't. "Just stay still," Slone said as he felt around on Carter's body. "I don't think you're hurt badly. I have called an ambulance. So just lie still till they get here. Slone stood up. He looked down on Carter. "But Sheriff, if you don't let this go. You're going to force me to have to kill you. So think about your family. Let it go!" Carter watched as Slone walked away and then slipped back into unconsciousness.

*

When Carter next opened his eyes, everything was blurry. His head was hurting, and he tried to move and felt pain all over his body. He then heard a familiar voice. "Well, you are alive."

Carter looked to his left, and as his eyes came into focus, he saw that the man standing next to his bed was Tusla County Sheriff Jim Dorsey. Carter laid his head back down on his pillow. Dorsey came a step closer. "Ya know, I get a call at home saying that one of my men had been hit by a Mack truck in a car chase. So I take off out to the scene. They say the driver has already been taken to the hospital. I walked over to the car. To my surprise, it's not one of mine. It's a Limestone County, Texas patrol car. So I put two and two together and knew it just had to be you. Well, I figured you would be back in Central Texas by now. Not doing high-speed chases in my County. Now, give me a good reason why I should not arrest you?

Carter turned and looked at Dorsey. "Sheriff, I had to check it out for myself. I went and saw Maggy Slone." Dorsey shakes his head as he looks hard at Carter, he says. "After I specifically ask you not to!" There was a long silence. Then Carter said. "Yes, I did. But I had to know for sure after talking to her. My gut was telling me she was lying. So I followed her. She went to a park and met him there. I tried to apprehend him. He saw me coming, took off, ran to her car, and sped off. I got in my patrol car and followed him. Just as I was catching up, he sped through a yellow light. I followed and got hit." Dorsey looked down and then away and back at Carter. "So you're telling me that you followed Maggie Slone to meet her dead son, then chased him across town till you had an accident running a red light."

Carter then looks up at him and says. "Yes, that's what I'm telling you. Oh, and I left out the part where he came back and pulled me out of the car." Dorsey then looks down at Carter. "This story gets crazier by the minute. Ok, for starters, let's say it is him. Why didn't you call my people for backup?" Carter then says. "There was no time. If I had waited, he would have been gone."

Dorsey then turns and walks toward the window, looks out for a moment, then turns and faces Carter. "Ok, this is how this is going to go. When you get out of here. You go straight back to Texas. I will check into this and keep you informed. Understood?" Carter frowned. "But Sheriff, this is my case! I have been trailing this guy for months!

Dorsey then angrily says. "I don't care! I can't have a loose cannon, out-of-state Sheriff, going off half-cocked in my County! Understood? Carter looks over at Dorsey for a moment and then says. "Ok, Sheriff. I'll go home."

Dorsey says, "Good. I will let you know if I find anything." He then turns and walks out the door.

*

A few hours later, Sheriff Dorsey was back in his office, sitting behind his desk as he tried to get some paperwork done, but he was having problems keeping focused. His mind kept coming back to his conversation with Sheriff Carter this morning. Was Jake Slone still alive? At first, he had thought it had just been a big mistake. But he didn't see Carter coming all the way here if he thought he was really dead.

But he and Jake had been friends. Surely he would have contacted him if he was alive. Well, this was in his head now. He was going to have to check it out.

He turned his chair around to his computer and logged in. He looked up traffic cams. He pulled up to the intersection where the accident happened. He then punched in the time of the accident. He saw the Mack truck hit Carter's patrol car. Wow, he was lucky to be alive. He then went back and looked at the car that went through the light just before. The picture at one angle showed what looked like a male driver. But it was too blurry to really tell anything. Then he pulled the plate number off the car. He then ran it through the system. He quickly got a hit. It was registered to Maggie Slone.

Ok, now he sat back in his chair. So Carter was chasing Maggie's car. He could tell from the picture that it was a male, not Maggie, driving.

Ok, wait. Carter said that Slone pulled him out of the car. So he pulled up another angle. He saw Carter's car flip over and come to rest. A few minutes later, he sees a man walking up to the car, opens the door, and pulls Carter out. The man was tall and had the same build as Slone. He lays Carter on his back and checks him. He sees Carter try to pull his gun. The man stops him, takes the gun, and slides it away. The man then turns and walks away.

Dorsey just sits there trying to take in what he has just seen. He then thinks of something. He pulls up the 911 recording of the reported accident. A few moments later, he finds it. He hits play. As he listens to the tape, he hears a familiar voice. It was the voice of a man he grew up with. The voice of a respected war hero. And if Sheriff Carter was right. The voice of a killer. But one thing he knew for sure. It was the voice of Jake Slone!

Chapter 9

After listening to the 911 tape, Sheriff Dorsey knew he had to see Maggie Slone. He walked out of his office and over to his secretary's desk. She looked up at him and smiled. He returned the smile and said, "I'm going to be out of the office for a while. If anybody needs me, have them call me." She looked up and said, "Will do, Sheriff."

He then walked out to his car and got in. He didn't normally leave without giving details about where he would be, but he was not ready to tell everybody in the office what he was doing, not yet anyway.

The drive would take him about 20 minutes. That would give him some time to think about what he was going to say to her. If she had met Jake at that park, and everything that Carter had told him, and what he had found himself. It looked like she did. Then she, of course, knew Jake was alive. He hoped she would be upfront with him.

Pulling up in front of the house, he got out. Walking up the drive, he saw a pickup parked in the driveway. He stopped, took out his phone, and took a picture of the license plate. He might need that later. Knocking on the door. A few moments later, the door opened, and Maggie Slone smiled at him. "Jim Dorsey, I haven't seen you in a while. Come in." Dorsey smiled back. "Hey, Maggie, how have you been?" Dorsey said as he walked past her inside. They walked down the hall to the living room. Dorsey looked around but didn't see Mitchelle.

"How is Mitchelle doing?" Dorsey asks. They both sat down on the couch. Maggie then said. "Well, she is not having a good day. But we did get some good news. They have found her a heart. They are bringing it into the Oklahoma Surgical Hospital here in Tulsa. We are headed there early in the morning." Dorsey smiles. "That's great news." Maggie nods. "Yes, it was an answer to a prayer." Dorsey smiles, grabs Maggie's hand, and gives it a squeeze.

He knows he needs to explain why he is here, but doesn't want to spoil Maggie's upbeat mood. He knows how hard it has been on Maggie with Mitchelle so sick.

She then looks over at him and says. So what brings you by, Jim? His smile fades away. He knows he can't avoid it any longer. "Well," Dorsey says. Not really knowing how to start. "It's about Jake. I hear a Sheriff from Texas came to see you the other day. He thinks Jake is alive." Maggie nods her head. "Yes, he came by and we talked for a few minutes. It was all a big misunderstanding." Dorsey then moved forward on the couch. "I talked to Sheriff Carter this morning. "He says he followed you to the park, and you met Jake, and he chased him, and he wound up getting into an accident." Her eyes got big. There was a moment of silence. She then said. "I hope nobody was hurt?" Dorsey shook his head. "Sheriff Carter is in the hospital, but he is going to be ok." "Good." She said.

Dorsey then looked over at her and said. "Ok, getting back to the chase." He pulled a picture from his coat pocket and held it up for her. "This is the car that Carter was chasing." She looks at it. "The plates are registered to you. A man is driving. He looks a lot like Jake." She lowers her head but says nothing. "The man driving your car comes back and pulls Carter out of the car." He pulls another picture out and shows it to her. He also makes a 911 call. The voice is Jake's."

He pauses for a moment. "I have known you and Jake for a long time. He was my best friend. You were like a 2nd mother to me. I think it's pretty clear. Jake is alive. I need you to be straight with me. I'm not sure what's been going on with him or what he is mixed up with. I want to help him. But to do that. I got to know what's going on."

She looks over at him with tears in her eyes. "I thought he had been killed in Afghanistan. I buried him. I mourned for him. I took on the responsibility of raising Mitchelle. We both thought he was dead till about a year ago. He just shows up at our door one day. All he would say was that he got word that Mitchelle was sick. He wanted to help her. He wouldn't say much about where he had been, only that we needed to keep it a secret. Over the next few months, he stayed here with us. Mitchell got sicker and needed some treatment and meds. That we didn't have the money for, he said he would take care of it. He took a job somewhere and left. He would send back money, large sums of cash. I didn't know where he got it, and I didn't ask. All I cared about was getting Mitchelle what she needed. When he did come back, he never stayed here. He would just show up from time to time."

There was a long silence, both letting what she said sink in. Then Maggie said. "I don't know what happened to him in Afghanistan, but he came back changed. But deep down, he is still my boy." Dorsey nodded. "Do you have any idea where I can find him?" "No." She said. Dorsey stood up. "He was driving your car. Is the truck parked out front his?" She looked up at him. "Yes." He then said. "Can I take a look at it?" She stands up. "Yes. Whatever you need." She wipes away tears. "Please help him." He starts toward the door. "He turns back to her. "I will, Maggie. I promise."

He opens the front door and walks out. Maggie closes it behind him. He walks over to the truck in the driveway. He looks it over. It's an older truck. Blue and white two-tone Ford. He looks in the bed and sees a bag. He opens it and finds clothes. He must have been planning a trip. He opens the door and looks inside. It looks clean and well taken care of. He gets in and sits behind the wheel. He pulls down the visor on the driver's and passenger sides. Nothing there. He opens the glove box. He finds a flashlight and some insurance and registration papers. He looks at the papers. It's registered to Maggie. He closes the glove box. He feels under the seat. He feels something, and he bends over, looks, and pulls out a large file.

He sits back in the seat and looks at the thick yellow file folder with about an inch worth of papers in it. He opens it up. It on a Navy Captain Marvin Briggs. Looking through it. It was just about everything you would need to know about Captain Briggs. It had everything, looking through it, every metal, every commendation. Every command he ever had. Then there was personal stuff. His divorce. Drinking problems, oh, and it gets interesting in the end. Suspected contact with the Russians. He sits back in the truck seat.

Why would Jake Slone have this obviously classified file on Captain Briggs? Who could Slone be working with to have this kind of stuff? It was starting to get scary to think about.

It looks like Captain Briggs is stationed at the Naval Air Station in Dallas, Texas. He had a feeling that if he found Captain Briggs, he would find Jake Slone.

*

John Carter set up on his hospital bed. They had just released him. His whole body was sore and hurt. But the only real damage was a cut on his temple around his hairline that took about six stitches and a slight concussion. God had obviously been looking over him. It could have been so much worse. Not to mention that Slone could have easily killed him. He was lucky to be alive.

He had called Carolyn. He had downplayed the whole thing. He didn't want to upset her. He would fill her in on the details when he got home. She wanted to dive up here to get him. But he didn't want her to miss any work. Her job was on shaky grounds as it was, because of him. He didn't want to make things worse. He also called Deputy Roberts and told him about the totaled patrol car. The County commissioners were going to love that. He didn't want to think about what it was going to cost to get it hauled back to Groesbeck. But there was equipment in it that they might could still use.

They had cut his clothes off in the ER, so all he had to put on were some hospital scrubs. He looked a sight: scrubs, boots, and a Silver belly cowboy hat. If he weren't so sore, it might be funny. Right now, he didn't even care what he looked like. He put his badge in his pocket, picked up his shoulder holster gun belt, set down in the wheelchair, and they started wheeling him out.

When he got outside, there was a taxi waiting for him. He stood up and winced in pain. He thanked the nurse and got in the taxi. The taxi driver gave him a funny look when he saw how he was dressed. Then a scared look when he saw his gun. He pulled his badge out of his pocket and showed it to the driver to put him at ease.

They drove to his hotel. Getting out, Carter paid the driver and made his way back to his room. Opening the door, he entered and placed his gun belt and hat on the table. He sat down on the bed and took his boots off.

He lies back on the bed. He had messed up big time. Why had he tried to chase him through that red light? She should have just stopped. He was in his mother's car. He had a tracker on it. He could have dropped back and followed at a safe distance. He was just right there within my grasp. I just got caught up in the moment. I was not thinking. Stupid mistake. He was lucky it didn't get him killed. Now he was out of range and in the wind again. All he had to show for it was a concussion, six stitches, a sore body, and last but not least, a wrecked patrol car.

His brother Brian was coming to get him. He was also the Pastor of his Church, so he was sure to get a lecture from him as both a Pastor and a brother.

He closed his eyes. The next thing he knew, there was a knock on the door. Jerking awake, he jumped up, grabbed his gun, and took it out of the holster. He looked through the peephole. He saw his brother Brian knocking on the door. He opened the door. He looked at Brian. "Thanks for coming, brother." Stepping back, Brian entered the room, taking a long, hard look at John. "You look awful! Are you ok?"

Carter slowly walked back to the bed and sat down. "Ya, I'm ok. Just a little cut and sore body. I'm fine." Brian pulled out a chair at the table and sat down. "You don't look fine. Obviously, there was more to this accident than what you told Carolyn. What happened?" Carter looks back at his brother and says. "I found him, I found Jake Slone." Brian looks over at him with a confused look on his face. "Jake Slone, is that the guy who was killing all those people and set fire to Fort Parker?" Carter nods his head.

"I came up here to talk to his mother. After talking to her, I felt she knew more than what she was saying. So I put a tracker on her car. I followed her to a park where she met him. I chased him. He got in her car, and I followed him. He sped through a yellow light, and I tried to follow and got hit by a Mack truck and flipped my car." Brian looks at John. "You could have been killed." Carter smiles. "Well, this is where it gets weird. Slone circles back and pulls me out of the car. Tell me to let it go, and if I don't, he is going to have to kill me. Then I pass out and wake up in the hospital."

Brian then says. "Ok, that is weird. He could have easily killed you, and why didn't you call for backup?" Carter stands up and starts pulling the hospital scrubs off. "Well, it gets weirder still. The local Sheriff knows Slone. Went to school with him. Served in the Navy with him. He is convinced he is dead and told me not to bother his mom. Then came to see me in the hospital and really lit into me for going to see his Mom and getting in a car chase in his County. So there will be no help there."

Brian stood up. "Ya know this could only happen to you." Brian walked over to the nightstand and looked in the drawers. "What are you looking for?" Carter asked. Brian looks back at him and says. "A Bible." As he pulls one out of the drawer and holds it up. Carter pulls his pants on."You didn't bring yours with you?" Brian rolls his eyes. Yes, of course, I brought it with me. But I left it in the car. I was not expecting you to be in dire need of prayer! I want the power of God's word in my hands when I do it."

Brian walks over to Carter and puts his hand on his shoulder. Carter looks at him. "Can this wait till I finish getting dressed?" Brian looks back at him. "No. God doesn't care how you're dressed." Carter protests no more and just bows his head.

Brian puts his hand back on John's shoulder. "Dear Heavenly Father. Thank you for looking over John and keeping your protective hand over him. Please lead and guide him and help him through this troubling time. Please bless him, lord, and keep him safe. Please give him healing in his body. Take away the soreness and discomfort. In the powerful name of Jesus. Amen."

John looks up and makes eye contact with his brother. "Thank you. I know I don't say it enough. But I really appreciate you and your prayers." Brian smiles. "Thank you. But you know you can talk to God yourself. You don't need me to do it for you. Share your feelings and worries. Put your trust in God. Let him carry the load." John smiles and nods.

John finishes getting dressed, and they gather his stuff. Carter puts his badge in his pocket, puts on his shoulder holster, checks the load on his 38, and holsters it. He then looks and sees the small 9mm ankle holster he normally wears around his left boot. But he is just too sore to bend over and put it on, so he just puts it in his bag.

They grab his stuff and head out the door. Now, he has about six hours to think of what he is going to tell Carolyn and the County Commissioners about what just happened.

Chapter 10

Jake Slone navigated the downtown Dallas traffic. He hated driving in a big city this time of day. He found a parking spot and quickly took it. He checked the load in his 9mm and put it back in the holster, under his jacket. Getting out, he walked behind the car and up on the sidewalk. He looked over at the bullet holes in the back window of his Mom's car. He needed to get that fixed. It drew attention to the car.

He started walking down the street. He was meeting Nathan Hunter. He needed to fill him in on his cover being blown. Carter knew who he was now. He could never go back home now, just when Mitchelle needed him most.

Walking down Houston Street, he wondered why Hunter had picked this of all places to meet. He stopped and crossed the street onto Elm Street. There on the corner of Houston and Elm, he stopped and looked up at the building he faced. Just like every other person who walked by here. It was the most famous building in Dallas. The Texas School Book Depository. He walked over to a bench and sat down. As he looked around Dealey Plaza, he could see at least six better places to shoot than the Depository.

Why would Oswald, a trained Marine, wait till the motorcade had passed and was moving away to shoot? That didn't make any sense. He should have shot as soon as they turned onto Elm and coming toward him. No Marine makes that mistake.

Then he is going to run down five flights of stairs. Stops on the 2nd-floor break room and buys a Coke. Then escapes by way of bus and taxi. Nobody is that stupid! He was what he said he was a patsy.

He knew Hunter was there before he saw him. He could just feel him. He came around from behind and sat down. He looked over at Slone. "How's it going, Jake?" Slone looked over his shoulder at the man standing behind the bench. Hunter then said. "This is Jeff Spencer, he is with me. An extra pair of eyes never hurts."

Slone nods. "I ran into a little problem leaving Tulsa yesterday. It seems that the Sheriff from Limestone County, Texas, John Carter, has somehow discovered my identity. He came to see my mother. She didn't tell him anything, but he followed her to meet me. He chased me. He was in an accident. I got away clean." Hunter frowned. "Did he survive the accident?" "Yes," Slone said.

Hunter sat back and crossed his legs. After a moment of silence, he says. "Well, I guess we will have to take care of the Sheriff." Slone shakes his head. "No, that won't be necessary. I got away clean." Hunter looks over at him. "We will have to move your family. Get everybody new identities." Slone nods. "Ya, I know."

Hunter smiles and pats Slone on the shoulder. "But I do have some good news. I made some calls and we have found Michelle a heart. It's headed to Oklahoma Surgical Hospital as we speak." Slone smiles big and reaches over to hugs Hunter. "That's great! I knew I could count on you." Slone sets back. Hunter smiles. "Well, I just did what I could do, and we got lucky." Slone smiles back. "Well, thank you. I will forever be in your debt."

Hunter then says. "Well, we still have a job to do." "Yes," Slone says. "I'm starting to prep work tonight. "Good," Hunter says.

They both sat back for a moment. Slone looks around and says. "So tell me, Nathan, you got connections. What really happened here? Hunter looks around. "Well, even with my connection. That's way above my pay grade." Both men stand up. Slone looks over at him. "I'm thinking, multiple gunmen. The fire escape on the Dal-Tex building, the roof of the Dallas County Record building, the Depository, and of course the Grassy Knoll."

Hunter looks over at Slone. "You may be right. But we will probably never know for sure. Not in our lifetime anyway." Slone turns and starts to walk away. Hunter calls to him. "So, Jake, if you were doing it alone. How would you do it?" Slone walks two steps back toward Hunter, looks around, and says. "One shot from behind the picket fence on the Grassy Knoll. Make my escape over the railroad tracks to a car waiting." Slone then turns and walks away.

Spencer, standing behind the bench, comes around and stands next to Hunter. Hunter looks at him and says. "We need to take care of that, Sheriff. He could be a thorn in my side. I will get you his info. I need you to handle it." The Spencer nods. "No problem, boss."

Spencer then looks over at Hunter. "You must really have connections to get a heart for that girl. That's amazing." Hunter watches Slone walk away and says. "Well, I did make a call. But the heart was already in the works. I really didn't have anything to do with it. But Slone doesn't need to know that. Him thinking he owes me can work to my advantage. It was not the first time I had played that card with him.

*

(Afghanistan 10 years earlier)

Jake Slone laid in his hospital bed. He had tried to sleep the last few hours but couldn't. Just too much going on. He didn't see how things could get any worse. The raid had gone bad. They had walked right into an ambush. Jessica and 15 of his men were dead! He was the only survivor. Now somebody was setting him up. They had made it look like he had sold out his men.

He lowered his head and wept. He couldn't believe she was gone. He heard a knock on the door. Looking up, he saw a Navy Lieutenant walking in. The man walked over to his bed and said. "Lieutenant Commander Slone?" Slone nodded his head and said. "Yes." The man then said. "I'm Lieutenant Morris, your JAG Lawyer." He walked over, shook hands with Slone, then pulled up a chair and sat down. He opened up his folder and looked at it for a moment. "Ok, Commander, it looks like you're going to be charged with aiding the enemy, 15 counts of murder, and most likely treason. But that charge has not been filed yet. They will wait till we get back to the United States to do that. You will be formally charged in the morning and flown back to the U.S. as soon as your doctors say you can fly. I will accompany you back. When we get there, I'm sure another lawyer with more experience will be assigned to you. This will be a very high-profile case. You will get the best lawyer we have, in the meantime. I will advise you not to say anything to anybody. No friendly talk to nurses, doctors, or anything. I can't stress this strongly enough! Do you understand?" Slone looked over at him and said. "Yes."

Lieutenant Morris then closed his folder and stood up. "Good." Shaking hands again. Morris starts toward the door, and he turns. "I will be back in the morning when they charge you. I'm sorry, wish I had better news." Slone says. "Thank you."

Morris leaves, and Slone lays his head back on his pillow. He thinks for a few minutes. He then reaches over, opens the nightstand drawer, and pulls out the phone Nathan Hunter gave him. He looks at the one number that is programmed into it. After a long moment, he hits the call button "Hunter." The voice on the other end says. "Mr. Hunter," Slone says, then pauses for a moment. "I'm In!" "Good," Hunter said. "You made the right choice. I will take care of everything." "Thank you," Slone says, ending the call.

Hunter lowers the phone from his ear and smiles. He looks and sees Lieutenant Morris walking down the hall toward him. "Good Job," Hunter says. He then turns to the two men standing with him, known as Captain Lewis and Agent Dunn. "He took the bait. Another performance won't be necessary." Hunter said. Lewis turns to him and says. "You think he will work out." Hunter smiles. "Oh yes! With his skill set and survivor's guilt, plus his hatred for O'mar Alead, he is going to be a very valuable asset for a long time!

*

(Present day)

Jake Slone pulled up outside the local bar and grill that Captain Marvin Briggs is said to hang out at every night. He had gotten here a little early. He wanted to be here when Briggs arrived. He ordered and ate, and just as he finished, Briggs walked in, still dressed in his Navy blues, he must have come straight from the base. Judging from how he was walking, it looked like he had already been hitting the bottle. He sat down alone at a table, and the waitress approached him and called him by name. She left and came back with a drink. Looked like Jack and Coke. He moved closer to him and sat at the bar just across from his table.

He sat there for a while, pretending to watch a baseball game on the TV on the wall, but really keeping a close eye on Briggs. When Briggs got up and moved toward the restroom, Slone made his move. He got up and turned quickly, and bumped into Briggs. "Oh, excuse me, " Slone said. Briggs frowned but didn't say anything, just heading on to the restroom.

Slone pretends to have dropped something, bends over, and places a listening device under the table that Briggs was setting. He turns and sits back down at the bar. He takes Briggs's phone, which he lifted off of him when he bumped him. He then takes out another phone and searches until it finds Briggs's phone. Then he hits clone data. Briggs's phone starts downloading its data to the clone phone. It takes about a minute and is done. He reaches and tosses the phone on the seat of Briggs' table. He will think he just dropped it.

Now he doesn't have to sit as close. He moves to the other side of the bar. Still close enough that he can see the table. About 20 minutes later, two men come in and look around till they find him. They walk over to the table. Slone places the earbud in his ear so he can hear them as the men walk up. The three men shake hands and greet each other, and all sit down. They engage in some small talk. The two men are definitely speaking with a Russian accent, though they are trying to cover it.

One of the men asks Briggs. "Do you have what we have talked about?" Briggs takes a sip of his drink. "I can get it. It will take a few days." The man looks over at Briggs. "When exactly? And where?" Briggs takes out a piece of paper and a pen and writes something down. He hands the paper to them. "This is the address of my place out in the country, just south of Waxahachie in Ellis County. Meet me there at 2 pm next Sunday. I'm assuming you will have what I have asked for?" The two men look at each other and back at Briggs. "Yes, we will have it." Briggs smiles and takes a drink. "Then we have a deal, Gentlemen. The three men stand up and shake hands. The two Russians leave, Briggs sits back down, and orders another drink.

Slone watches as Briggs eats dinner and has several drinks. He looks around. He keeps getting this uneasy feeling, kind of like a sixth sense. He sometimes gets these feelings right before things go really wrong. He looked around and saw nothing out of the ordinary.

A few minutes later, Briggs paid his bill and walked toward the door. Slone waited a few minutes. He had gotten everything he needed for now. There was no need to follow him.

He paid his bill and walked out the front door. He had parked down the street. So he made the walk down to his car. He got that uneasy feeling again. He knows better than to keep ignoring this feeling. He ducks into an alley and ducks down behind a trash dumpster. He reaches behind his back and grabs the handle of his 9mm, but waits to pull it out. He sees the silhouette of a man turning the corner into the alley. He cautiously takes a few steps and stops.

Slone then stands up and takes a step out into the light. "Well, Sheriff, I am impressed. Don't know how you found me here. The man then steps out into the light. He takes a long look at Slone. "Well, you got the job right but the person wrong." Sheriff Jim Dorsey says as he takes a few steps closer. He smiles. "You're looking good, Jake! For a guy who has been dead for 10 years!" Slone takes his hand off his gun and lowers it to his side. "Hey, Jimbo. I would ask what you are doing here. But I have a feeling that you have been talking to Sheriff Carter."Dorsey nods his head. "Ya, that's right, Jake. He told me some really disturbing things. I told him he was wrong. You were dead. You were a war hero. I told him to stay away from your Mom. Then I took a look at the traffic cam of Carter's accident, and low and behold. There you are. My best friend alive and well. So, think maybe you can explain some of that?"

Slone steps closer to Dorsey and looks up at him. "It's a long story, Jim. But I did what I had to do." Dorsey shakes his head. "Oh no. You've got to do better than that." Slone then says. "I can't go into details, Jim. You already know too much, just knowing I'm alive." Dorsey gives him an angry look. "What about Mitchelle? What about your Mom? How could you just walk away from them? Tell me something. Make me understand." Slone looks down, then back at Dorsey. "Leaving Mom and Mitchelle was the hardest thing I have ever done. But believe me when I tell you. The alternative was worse. Dorsey moves a step closer. "What could possibly be worse than that?" He asks. "I can't go into it. I don't expect you to understand. But believe me. The best thing for you, me, Mom, and Mitchelle is for you to forget you ever saw me. Remember me the way I was."

Slone turns and starts to walk away. Dorsey pulls his gun and points it at Slone. "You're coming back with me, and we are going to figure this all out!" Slone turns and looks at Dorsey for a long moment. "Jim, one thing I have learned over the last 10 years is how to read people's eyes. Look into their souls and know what they are going to do. We both know that you're not going to shoot me. We have been through too much together. Go home."

Slone turned and started walking away. Dorsey lowered his gun. Slone then stopped and turned to Dorsey. "Mitchelle is having her surgery soon. Can you be there for her?" Dorsey nodded. "Ya, I can do that." Slone smiled. "Thanks, Jimbo. Take care." He then turned and walked into the night.

Chapter 11

John Carter and his brother Brian pulled up in front of Carter's house in Groesbeck. It had been a long drive. But Carter had enjoyed spending the time with his brother. They had been close growing up. Even though they lived in the same town, less than a mile apart. They both had such busy lives that they never seemed to get a chance just to talk.

They both get out, and Carter gets his bag out of the back seat. Brian walks around to the passenger side of the car. Carter says. "Come in and let's get some coffee." Brian smiles. "I'd better get on home. I have been gone long enough. Are you going back to work tomorrow?" Carter shakes his head. "Oh, yeah. I'm going to have some explaining to do."

Brian extends his hand to shake. Carter takes his hand and then pulls him in for a hug. "Thank you for everything, brother," Carter says. "Anytime, brother. I will come by and check on you tomorrow." Brian says. Carter smiles. "Pray for me?" Brian smiles as he walks back around the car. "I always do, John. Love Ya." As Brian gets back in the car, Carter waves. "Love you too, brother."

Carter picks up his bag and walks toward the door. Opening and going inside, he sees Becky standing at the end of the hall. She smiles big as she comes toward him. "Daddy, I'm so glad you're ok and home!" She gives him a long, hard hug and kiss on the cheek. At about that time, Tom comes around the corner. "Hey, Dad," Tom says as he hugs him, reaches up, and takes off Carter's cowboy hat. "Wo Dad, that's a nasty looking cut on your head, and your eyes look kinda black." Carter takes his hat from Tom and puts it on the rack. "Ya, I know I look a little rough."

The kids step away, and he looks to see Carolyn walking toward him. She gives him a long hug and a brief kiss. She turns to the kids. "Why don't y'all set the table for dinner and wash up. I need to talk to your father. She walks toward the bedroom. Carter picks up his bag. Tom turns back and speaks softly. "She referred to you as your father. That's not good, Dad." Carter nods. "Ya, I know, son. Get cleaned up."

Carter walks into the bedroom and puts his bag on the bed. He looks over at Carolyn. "You could have gotten yourself killed! You know that?" She says. "Yes, I know. I'm sorry." She walks over and takes a look at the cut on his head. "What were you thinking? Going after a known killer, out of your jurisdiction, out of state. With no backup!" Carter turned, sat on the bed, and looked up at her. "When I went up there, I thought it was just to interview his mother. Things just got quickly out of hand."

She sits down on the bed beside him. "I can't live like this, John. You're obsessed with catching this guy! It's going to get you killed! You're a small-town Sheriff. You're suppose to find missing cows. Stolen lawnmowers and maybe a marijuana bust from time to time. But not track a killer to another state!" There was a long silence, then he said. "I know the things that have happened here last year are not supposed to happen here. But they did happen here! I owe it to the ones that died and to their loved ones, like that kid Steven Smith. To do everything I can to bring him justice. She stands up and turns to him. "Ok, John. I just hope it doesn't cost you your family or your life." She kisses him on the forehead and turns and walks out.

*

The next morning, Carter jerked awake. He had hit the snooze button when it went off and went back to sleep. He jumped up, turned the light on, and headed to the restroom. There was a wet towel on the dirty clothes hamper. Carolyn must have gotten up and out early. He must have slept really hard. He looked in the mirror. The man, looking back, looked a mess. He had a cut on the head, black eyes, and he was so sore he could hardly move.

He shaved, cleaned up, and got dressed. Buttoning up his Sheriff's Department white shirt, he returned to the mirror. Well, he looked somewhat better. But not much. Oh well, it would have to do. Putting his gun belt on, he took his 38 revolver out of the safe, checked the load, and placed it in his holster. Then he placed his badge on his shirt and headed out of the bedroom.

When he got to the kitchen, he saw Tom sitting at the table eating Cap'n Crunch cereal out of the box. He looked up. "Hey, Dad. How are you feeling?" Carter walks over to the cabinet and takes out a coffee cup. "I'm fine. Just a little sore." He pours himself a cup of coffee, comes over to the table, and sits down. Tom says. "Mom says we are on our own for breakfast this morning. She is working in Waco today. She is dropping off Becky on her way out of town."

Tom takes another handful of cereal out of the box and shoves it in his mouth. Carter stares at him. "Did you wash your hands before you shoved them in that box?" Tom looks over at him with a surprised look on his face. "No. But I took a shower before I went to bed. I don't think I got dirty sleeping." Carter looks at Tom and rolls his eyes but says nothing. A moment later, Tom says. "Are you hungry, Dad? I can cook you a Pop-Tart or something." Carter smiles. "No son. But thank you."

About that time, a horn honks in front of the house. Tom jumps up, closes the cereal box, and puts it up. "That's my ride, Dad, Betty Ann Baxter. She got her license a few weeks ago." Tom throws his backpack over his shoulder. "She is smoking hot!" He nods and winks. "Later, Dad." He then heads toward the door.

A few minutes later, Deputy Greg Roberts pulls up in front of the house. Carter has been watching for him. He goes out and gets into the patrol car. Roberts looks over at him. "Morning, boss. You look like shit!" Carter turns with an annoyed look on his face. "Yes, I know. Thank you. Can you drive?"

They make the short drive to the Sheriff's Department. Neither one of them notices the black car parked down the street, which follows them and watches them walk inside.

Inside, everybody looks busy, but shift change was always busy. Carter speaks to several Deputies and makes his way to Nancy's desk. "Morning, Nancy, " he says. She looks up at him, and her smile disappears. "Oh, you don't look so good." Carter forces a smile. "It looks worse than it is."

He walks over and gets a cup of Nancy's Coffee. He pauses for a moment. He was wanting a cup of Nancy's god awful coffee. Could things get any worse? He walks into his office and sits down behind the desk. Deputy Roberts comes in and briefs him on what has been going on while he was gone. Carter tried to listen but didn't hear most of what Roberts was saying. His mind wandered to what had happened in the last few days. To finding Slone's mother, Slone getting away to Carolyn's ultimatum last night.

Roberts had stopped talking, and Carter looked up. "You ok? John." Roberts asks. Carter nodded. "Yes," Carter said. "Thank you for taking care of things while I was gone." Roberts stands up. "No problem," as Roberts turns to leave. Carter says. "Hey, Greg." Roberts stops and turns back to him. "I'm going to write a report on the Mike McKinney interview. The interview with Slone's mother and my encounter with him, and turn it all over to the F.B.I. We are going to let them handle it. Roberts nods and walks out.

Carter spent the next few hours writing his report. He sat back in his chair and threw his pen on the desk. He put everything he could think of into it, hoping it would help them.

He stood up and walked out of the office, into the bullpen, and over to Nancy's desk. She looked up. "Nancy, can you get me keys to a patrol car. Nancy reached in her desk and pulled out a set of keys.

"#23 and old but a good one." She says. He smiles. "Thank you, Nancy. I'm going out to the gun range. If you need anything, call." "Sure thing, Sheriff," she says as he walks away.

He finds his car and pulls out of the parking lot toward the range, he doesn't notice the man in the black car following him. He liked coming out to the range and shooting. When he was a boy, his Papaw would bring him out to the range and teach him how to shoot. He set up a target and shot a few rounds. He looked at the target. All the shots were in the center mass of the target. He looked at his old 38 revolver with his Papaw's J.D.C. initials on the handle. It still shot good.

He hears the door to the range open, and he looks to see his brother Brian walking toward him. "Hey, Brother," Brian says. "Hey," Carter says as he puts another target up and hits the button to move it back into place. He put his ear protectors on and handed a pair to Brian, who put them on. He fires four shots, pauses for a moment, and fires four more. He hits the button to retrieve the target. He looks at it. All shots in center mass.

Carter takes the target down. "That's good shooting," Brian says. Carter nods. Brian then looks over at his brother. "So, how did it go after you got home?" Carter turns back to him. "Well, it went about as bad as it could have gone. I'm about one screw up from losing my family. Poll numbers still not looking good. So I could lose re-election, and on top of all that. Slone is still out there somewhere. Other than that, everything is great. Brian puts his hand on Carter's shoulder. "Joh,n I'm sure Carolyn will settle down. She was just upset. Poll numbers are just that, numbers. They change every day. I'm sure you'll get a break in the case soon. You just need to put it in God's hands and let him carry the load. Carter nods. "I hope you are right."

He then put another target up. He hands Brian his 38 revolver. "Ok, let's see if you still got it." Brian puts the gun down. "No, John. I don't do that anymore. You know this. I sure can't shoot a target that is a silhouette of a person." Carter then takes the target down, looks through his targets, and puts up a plain round target. "Ok, now you happy." He hits the button to send it back and holds the gun up for Brian to take. "You learned to shoot just like I did with this very gun. That was Papaw's. I won't tell."

Brian puts on his ear protectors and takes the gun. He loads eight rounds. Takes aim and fires four rounds, and then four more. He puts the gun down on the table. Carter hits the return button. He looks over at Brian. "You enjoyed that, you know it." Brian gives a slight smile. They look at the target. All shots are within 3 inches of the center. Carter looks at the target and then at his brother. Brian is unable to fight back a bigger smile. "You still got it!" Carter says.

Brian takes his ear protector off. "Well, I need to go. I just wanted to check on you," Carter smiles. "Thanks, brother." Brian starts toward the door, stops, and turns back. "Put it in God's hands, John. I'm praying for you." Brian leaves, and Carter fires a few more rounds.

Carter packs his stuff up and heads to his car. It's time to get back to the real world. He starts the car and heads out. He needs to run by the house to pick up his notes on his trip to Tulsa. He wants to turn everything he has over to the F.B.I. Maybe it would be some help. As he pulls into his driveway and gets out, he doesn't notice the back car pass by.

Unlocking the front door, he walked inside and straight to his home office. He found the notes he was looking for and quickly looked over them. He found a yellow envelope and placed the notes inside. He got up and headed out into the hall toward the front door.

In the hallway, Carter is startled to see a man standing just inside the front door, holding a gun in one hand and a rope in the other. Carter's hand quickly drops to his gun. But the man quickly brings his gun to bear, pointing it at Carter. "I wouldn't do that if I were you, Sheriff." Carter slowly backs his hand away from his gun. The man walks closer and takes Carter's gun out of his holster. "Who are you and what do you want?" Carter says. The man looks at Carter. "Who I am is not important. Turn around." Carter turns, and the man takes his handcuffs off his belt and puts them on Carter. "What's this about?" Carter says louder this time. The man loops the rope around the light fixture and ties it to a doorknob. The man then says. "Let's just say you should have just left it alone."

The man then ties the end into a noose. Carter is now getting the idea of what is fixing to happen. "You're working for Slone?" The man smiles. "Not exactly." Carter looks over at the clock. The kids would be home any minute. "Not here!" Carter shouts. "Take me someplace else. But not here!" The man turns to Carter and says. "You're not in a position to be making demands, Sheriff." He then puts the noose around Carter's neck. "Carter then says. "I don't want my kids to find me like this! Don't do this. Not here." The man then pulls a chair over to him. "I'm sorry. But this is how it has to be. Now get up on the chair." Carter gives the man an angry look. "Fuck you! I'm not getting on that chair." The man takes out his gun and points it at Carter. "I said, get on the chair." Carter looks the man straight in the eye and says. "And I said fuck you! Shoot me!"

The man takes a step back and puts the gun in his belt. "Very well. We will do this the hard way." He goes over to the knob and takes the rope loose and pulls all the slack out of it. The noose tightens. Around Carter's neck, the man kept pulling on the rope. Carter is now up on his toes and starting to choke. The man ties off the rope, walks over, pulls the chair over, and places Carter's legs on it. Carter stands on the chair and is able to get a few breaths. The man looks up at Carter. "Now, why couldn't we have done that the easy way?"

About that time, they heard the front door opening. They both turn to look. Carter is terrified to see his son Tom coming in the door with his daughter Becky close behind. Carter sees the man reaching behind his back for his gun. Carter kicks up with his left leg and hooks it around the man's neck. He then brings his right leg over and hooks it around his left foot. He pulls the man to him and squeezes as hard as he can. He tries to yell for the kids to run, but the rope keeps cutting off his air. He sees Tom turn around and push his sister back out on the porch.

The man starts getting weaker and drops to his knees and then to the ground. The chair has been knocked over, so Carter is now hanging, unable to get any air at all now. Tom runs over, grabs his Dad by the legs in a big bear hug, and lifts him up. He yells, "Becky, get the rope!" Becky runs back inside and is shocked at what she sees. She runs over to the doorknob that the rope is tied to and pulls the slip knot hard. The rope comes loose, and Carter falls down on top of Tom, and they both fall to the ground.

Tom reaches up and loosens the rope around his Dad's neck. Carter lies there, gasping for breath. "Dad, are you alright?" Tom says. "Yes," Carter says as they both get to their feet. "There is a handcuff key in my pocket." Tom reaches into his pocket, pulls out his keys, and finds the handcuff key. He starts trying to take the cuffs off.

Becky yells, "Daddy!" Carter turns to see the man getting up on his hands and knees. Carter kicks as hard as he can, hitting the man just under his chin with the toe of his boot. The man falls back to the ground. Carter moves over the man and puts his foot on his back so he can't get back up. Tom then finishes taking the handcuffs off and hands them to him. Carter reaches down and puts the cuffs on the man.

Carter turns and looks at the kids. "Are you both okay? " he says in a very raspy voice. Becky comes over and hugs him. "I was so scared, Daddy. Are you OK?" Carter nods. Yes, I'm okay."

Carter sets the chair back up and then bends down, pulls the man to his feet, and sets him down in the chair. His nose is bleeding. Carter pushes the man's forehead back, making him look at him. He says in a still very raspy voice, "We have a lot to talk about!"

Chapter 12

Sheriff John Carter and his kids, Tom and Becky, pulled into his parking spot at the Limestone County Sheriff's Department. After what had just happened, there was no way he could leave them alone. They walked inside, and Nancy met them at the door. "Oh my gosh. Thank God y'all are alright." She gave Becky a hug.

Carter says to the kids. "Why don't you wait in my office?" Carter reaches into his pocket and takes out his wallet. "Here, get y'all something out of the vending machines." He hands Tom some cash. "Thanks, Dad," Tom says as they walk toward the break room. When they were out of earshot. Nancy says. "What happened?" Carter looks over at her. "This guy followed me in the front door and pulled a gun on me. He tried to hang me and make it look like a suicide. She looks at the burn marks on his neck. "Your voice sounds awful. Did you go to the E.R.? He shakes his head. "No. I'm fine. I want to get the kids here where I know it's safe."

They walked over to her desk and they both sat down. "Have you talked to Carolyn yet?" She says. "Yes, I called her. She is on her way home. She wouldn't wait for me to send somebody to get her." Carter said. "How's she handling it?" Nancy asks. "Carter looks up at her. "Not good. Not good at all."

Deputy Fox walks up and puts his hand on Carter's shoulder. "You ok?" Carter nods. "Ya, I'm fine. I had Roberts and Hayes take the suspect to the E.R. to get minor injuries looked at. Maybe broke a nose." Fox frowns. "He is lucky a broken nose is all." Carter looks over at him. "I want everything handled by the book. When they get here with him. I want him processed and fingerprinted. I want to know who this son of a bitch is."

Carter gets up and walks toward his office. Inside, Becky is sitting in a chair, staring out into space. She turns and looks at him with a sad look on her face. "Are you okay, baby?" Carter asked. She forces a smile. "Yes, Daddy." He walks over to her, puts his hand on the top of her head, and gently caresses her hair. He bends down and kisses her on the top of her head.

"I'm so sorry you had to go through what you did today. I wish I could change things." Becky looks up at him. "We are just glad you're okay, Daddy."

Carter looks over at Tom, sitting behind his desk with his feet propped up on the desk. Tom looks over at him as he takes a drink from his Dr. Pepper. "Hey, Dad. I found your stash of peanuts. Did you know that if you put peanuts into your bottle of Dr. Pepper, you get an amazing taste of both Dr. Pepper and the peanuts? It's just amazing. I can't believe I just invented this. I'm going to get a patent on this. There must be a lawyer in this building someplace. I'm going to be rich!" Carter smiles. "I don't think you invented that, Tom. People were doing that before I was born." Tom throws his head back. "Aw, Dad, really, nobody told me." Carter shakes his head. "Yes, afraid so, son, sorry."

About that time, the door opened and Carolyn came in. Becky jumps up, runs over to her mother, and hugs her. Carolyn holds her tight. "Thank God y'all are ok! I can't imagine what you have been through." Tom gets up and walks over to his Mother. "Ya know, Mom, I was the real hero here. Just saying." Carolyn looks over at Tom and grabs him in a big hug. After a long moment, they pull back. Tears are going down both Carolyn's and Becky's cheeks.

Tom holds up his Dr. Pepper bottle. "Mom, did you know putting peanuts in Dr. Pepper is awesome?" Carolyn smiles. "Yes, I knew that, Tom." Tom takes a drink and throws up his hands. "I just missed out on being rich."

Carolyn walks over to Carter and hugs him. "I'm glad you're ok too." She looks at the burn marks on his neck. "Have you been to the hospital?" Carter shakes his head. "No. I'm fine." She frowns. "You don't look fine with that cut on your head, two black eyes, and now rope burns on your neck." He tries to smile. "It looks worse than it really is," Carter says in a raspy voice. She gives him a hard look. "That voice sounds fine, too."

She looks over at the kids. "Can you give me a few minutes? I need to talk to your father." The kids start walking toward the door. Tom leans over and whispers in his Dad's ear, "She used father again, Dad. It's not good."

As soon as the door closes behind them, Carolyn says. "How can this happen, John? You brought this into our home! Our kids are not safe! You all three could have been killed! I can't live like this, John." Carter takes a step closer to her. "I don't know what's happening. But I'm going to make sure that you and the kids are safe." She jerks her head around. "Oh, really, John. How are you going to do that? Look at you. You can't even protect yourself." Carter takes a moment to pick his words carefully. "I'm going to do everything I can to get to the bottom of this and keep you and the kids safe. You have my word on that. I'm going to find y'all a place to stay for a few days. I'm going to post a deputy outside." She looks down and then back up at Carter. "For how long, John? You have no idea. It's not safe to be around you, John. I can't live like this. I love you, but we can't be anywhere near you. "I'm going to stay with my Mother for now." Carter nods his head. "Ok, I understand. It will get better. I will fix this." She turns and walks toward the door. She turns back. "Some things you can't fix, John," Carolyn says as she leaves.

Carter sits down at his desk and puts his head in his hands. There is a knock on the door, and Deputy Roberts comes in. "We got him set up in interrogation room one." Carter looks up. "Good, has he said anything?" "No," Roberts said. "Not a word." Carter stands up. "Ok, I'm going to talk to him. I will need you in there with me. Don't let me kill him."

He starts walking toward the door. "Oh, Carolyn and the kids are going to stay with her mother. I want somebody posted on them at all times. She may not like it. I don't care."

Carter and Roberts walk out of the office and toward the interrogation room, Deputy Billy Hayes meets them. Hayes hands Carter a file. "We got a quick hit on his prints. He was in the system. His name is Jeff Spencer, a 30-year-old former Army Ranger. Honorably discharged four years ago, and can't find anything else on him after that, like he fell off the face of the earth. But I need more time to look." "Ok, good," Carter says. "Keep digging." Hayes nods. "You got it, boss."

Carter and Roberts walk into the viewing room and can see Spencer threw the glass. Carter looks through the file Hayes gave him. "How do you go from an Army Ranger to a killer?" Carter asked. "Roberts takes the file and looks it over. "This doesn't say much. But it sure doesn't look like a killer." Carter looks at him through the mirror. "Slone's file didn't look like a killer either. That's one thing they have in common. At the house, I asked him if he was working for Slone. He said not exactly. So this is connected to Slone somehow. Let's do this."

They walk out of the viewing room and into the interrogation room. Spencer turns and looks at them. He is handcuffed to the table. Carter puts the file on the table and pulls up a chair across from Spencer. "Ok, Mr. Jeff Spencer." Carter looks him in the eye. "Yes, I know who you are. I have some questions for you." There is a moment of silence, and the two men look at each other. "Why were you trying to kill me?" Spencer says nothing. "Who do you work for?" Spencer says nothing. Carter looks at the file and then back at Spencer. "You have anything to say?" Spencer looks at him. "I would like a lawyer, my phone call, and maybe some water, please." Carter stands up. Now that he had officially lawyered up. That was the end of the interview. Carter looks down at him. I'm going to get to the bottom of this. Like you said, I just can't let it go. Carter turned to Roberts. "Let him make his phone call and get him a bottle of water." Carter and Roberts leave the room.

A few minutes later, Roberts returns with a water bottle and a cordless phone. He sets the water and phone down on the table, takes out his handcuff key, and removes the cuff from his right hand, leaving his left hand cuffed to the chair. "I will be back in a few minutes," Spencer nods. "Thank you." Roberts leaves the room and closes the door behind him.

Spencer picks up the water bottle, removes the top, and takes a drink. He sets it down and picks up the phone. He dials a number, and on the 3rd ring it is picked up. "Yes." The voice on the other end says. "This is Spencer. We have a caged bird situation." A moment of silence. "Understood." The voice says. "Initiate caged bird protocol." "Understood," Spencer says. "I will make sure everything is taken care of on my end." The voice says. Another long pause. "It's been an honor, sir," Spencer says. "The honor has been mine." The voice says. The line goes dead.

Spencer lays the phone down and reaches down with his free hand to his left boot. He works the heel back and forth until it comes off. He turns the loose heel upside down, and a small pill falls out into his right hand. He reaches up and puts it in his mouth, grabs the water bottle, and takes a long drink. A few moments later, he starts convulsing and foaming at the mouth, and he falls down on the table.

Roberts hears sounds coming from the interrogation room and runs back in. He sees Spencer with his head down on the table. He yells. "Code Blue!" He quickly moves and takes off Spencer's handcuffs off his left hand and lowers him to the floor. Carter and Deputy Hayes come into the room. "What's going on? " Carter says. Roberts looks up at him. "I found him unresponsive. He is not breathing, no pulse." Roberts starts doing CPR. Deputy Fox brings in the first aid box. Hayes starts to do mouth-to-mouth. Carter sees the foam coming out of Spencer's mouth. Carter stops him. "Use the mask and airbag."

The three of them take turns working on him until paramedics arrive. The paramedics look him over. He looks up at Carter. "I'm sorry, Sheriff, he is gone."

"Damn!" Carter says. He looks around and points to the phone on the table. "Do we know who he called?" Hayes picks up the phone. "Yes, we can pull a number." Carter looks over at Hayes. "Do we have ears on that line?" Hayes shakes his head. "No. For the first call, we always assume they are calling a lawyer. We always let them use the house phone." "Ok," Carter says. "Get the number. I'm betting it's a burner phone that's been discarded." Hayes pulls the number off the phone's history and writes it down. "I will see what I can find out on this." Hayes turns and leaves the room.

Carter then turns to Roberts. "Call Freestone County Sheriff Don Goodwin. Tell him we have a death in the jail. Brief him on what happened. Get him to send an investigation team over." Roberts nods. "We are not going to handle this in-house?" "No," Carter says. "With this guy trying to kill me, then turning up dead in the jail. No, we can't touch this. Seal this room off till they get here.

Carter walks back to his office. Setting behind his desk, he runs his hands through his hair. He sits back in his chair, trying to process what all has happened in the last few hours. How could things get any worse? Just when he thought he had a lead, it's gone. This Spencer guy he is connected to Slone somehow. He said as much at the house. But now he was back to square one.

*

Nathan Hunter pulled the phone away from his ear. He briefly looked at it before throwing it into a trash can. Jeff Spencer had been a good asset, and he hated to lose him. But that's how things worked in this business. He would have to look into it and see if there were any more loose ends he needed to clean up. If that pesky Sheriff was still alive, he would most likely have to deal with him again at some point. But for now, he would have to let things die down.

He walked across the parking lot and entered the cafe. Looking to his left, he could see a row of booths, and at the end, he saw Jake Slone sitting facing the door with a view out the window. Slone saw him come in and watched him walk to the booth. "Hello, Nathan. Is everything ok?" Hunter sits down and says. "Yes, of course. Why?" Slone looks over at him. "I saw you on your burner phone, then you discarded it." Hunter looked over at Slone. "Yes, everything is fine. Just time to change phones. I will text you a new number. So, where are we at? Is it a go?" Slone looks around, then says. "Yes, it's going down tomorrow. I have got everything taken care of." "Good," Hunter says.

"Have you heard anything from your mother about Mitchelle?" Hunter asks. Slone smiles. Yes, the surgery went well, and everything looks great. I can't thank you enough for your help. You saved her life." Hunter looks back at him. I was glad I could help."

Hunter stands up. "Let me know when it is done." Slone nods. "I will." Hunter takes a step, then stops and turns back to Slone. "Ya know when this is done. We need to take a fishing trip somewhere." Slone smiles. "Ya, Nathan, that would be great." Hunter turns. "Take care, Jake." And walks away.

*

The intercom buzzed. Carter picked it up. "Nancy, whatever it is, can it wait? I really need some time to think. Oh really. Well, send him in." Carter hung up the phone with a surprised look on his face. He stood up and walked around the desk.

His office door opens, and a man walks in. Carter looks at him and smiles. "Sheriff Dorsey, Come in. This is a surprise. What brings you here?" The two men meet and shake hands. "Please have a seat," Carter says as the two men sit down in the two chairs in front of the desk. Dorsey looks at Carter. "Sheriff, I owe an apology. You were right, Jake

Slone is alive. After I left you in the hospital, I checked the traffic cam at the accident. I got a good picture of him. I then went to see his mother. She confessed that he was alive, that she had known for about a year. So I searched his truck. The one he left behind when he took his mom's car. I found this file." Dorsey hands the file to Carter, who opens it up and looks at it. "It was on Captain Marvin Briggs, everything you need to know about him is in that file. So I make a trip to Dallas, where Briggs is stationed. The file says he likes to hang out at this bar after work. So I go there hoping to meet up with him. Guess who is also there. Yep, you got it, Jake Slone. So I watch him, watching Briggs. When Slone leaves, I confront him. He tells me nothing about where he has been or what he is doing. He says I know too much already. He goes to leave. I pull my gun to stop him. I couldn't do it. He was my best friend.

But I also couldn't just stand by and let him kill Captain Briggs. I think something is going to go down this weekend at Briggs Farm just outside Waxahachie, Texas. I tried calling Briggs' office. They blew me off. Didn't take me seriously. So I have come to you."

"Wow," Carter says. "Let me fill you in on what's happened to me. "I get home, and a man tries to kill me in my home. Tries to hang me to make it look like a suicide." Carter shows him the rope burns on his neck. "We arrest the guy, bring him back here. He says nothing. Lawyers up. He makes a phone call and then kills himself in my interrogation room. I suspect he took a cyanide pill. I was just sitting here thinking of what the hell I was going to do next."

There was a moment of silence as both men looked at each other. Dorsey then says. "This is getting crazier by the moment." Carter nods. "Yes, tell me about it."

Dorsey stands up. "Well, Sheriff, I have to get back to Tulsa. I have been gone too long. Carter stands up, and they shake hands. Dorsey says. "I'm sorry, I didn't believe you, Sheriff. I hope this has been some help." "It has," Carter says.

Dorsey starts walking toward the door, stops, and turns back to Carter. "He was a good man and a good friend and served his country with honor. Try to take him alive if you can." Carter looks back and says. "I will do what I can. I will keep you posted." "Thank you," Dorsey says as he walks out the door.

Carter turns and sits down behind his desk. He looks through the Briggs file. It looks like he was going to make a trip to Waxahachie.

Chapter 13

Jake Slone heard his alarm go off for the 2nd time. He threw the covers back and set up in bed. He had not slept well. The people next door were noisy. You would think in a small town hotel, you would not have to put people right next to each other.

But he needed to be up anyway. He got up, showered, and got dressed. He went over his notes again. Everything he had gotten off Captain Briggs's phone. The exchange was going down at 2:00 pm this afternoon. Briggs had told them to meet him at his country place. He had scouted out the place yesterday. It was very secluded. Just goes to show what an amateur Briggs was. They could kill him, take the info, and keep the money. Things like this should be done in a very public place. But Briggs being stupid just made his job easier, also.

He took his sniper rifle out of the case and put it together. After making sure that everything was in good working order, he disassembled it and placed it back in the case. He picked up his 9mm and checked it. He put it in the holster and covered it with his shirt. He gathered the rest of his stuff, went to the lobby, and checked out.

He got into his car. It looked better now. He had gotten the window fixed yesterday. He drove down the street to the cafe. Inside, he walked down to the last booth and sat down where he could see the door and out the window. A waitress walked up and handed him a menu. He hands it back. "Two eggs scrambled, bacon toast, coffee." She smiled. "Got it. Coming right up." She said.

While, he was eating his breakfast. He couldn't help but think about Mitchelle. He had talked to his mother last night. She was doing really well. He wished he could be there for her. But that was not going to happen. Now that word was getting out that he was alive. They would come looking for him. That's the first place they will look, was with them. He could never go home again. He might never see them again. That broke his heart. But that was a choice he made a long time ago. But did he really have a choice? If it were not for Nathan Hunter, he would be rotting in a prison somewhere, or he would have been executed. At least this way, he had been able to provide for her. He could at least love her from afar. He should have let her go on thinking he was dead. At least that way, she could have been proud of her father, who died for his country. But when he heard she was sick. He had to come back. Now he was sure she hated him. Well, at least she was alive to hate him.

Maybe when this job is over, Hunter can get me a new identity. Maybe when Mitchelle recovers, she and Mom can join him. Well, that's what he was going to hope for anyway.

*

Sheriff John Carter met Deputies Greg Roberts and Billy Hayes at the Sheriff's Department. The few Deputies on duty were surprised to see them on a Sunday morning. They gathered up the few things they needed. On their way out to the car, Roberts says. "What do you think we are going to get into?" Carter stops at the car door. "I'm not sure. The Info I have tells me that this Captain Marvin Briggs could be a target of Slone's. We have to try to stop it or warn him, and maybe cross paths with Slone. That's why I want y'all with me. I don't want to go up against him alone again.

They get in the car and head out toward Waxahachie, Texas, a town small but still much larger than Groesbeck. It was also the County seat of Ellis County. He had tried to call Sheriff Jack Truman, but he could never get through to him. His office called back and said he would meet them at the Courthouse this morning. He was not looking forward to this meeting. He and Sheriff Truman didn't exactly get along well. They had never been friends, but things got really bad a few years ago when he had borrowed Deputy Mike Fields. He needed

Fields to work undercover in the McKinney Investigation. The one that started this whole mess. McKinney knew all the deputies in Limestone and Freestone Counties, so he had to use somebody from the outside. Truman didn't like the idea, to begin with, then when the opt ran longer than expected, he liked it even less.

Truman was in his fourth term as Sheriff, and he would most likely get re-elected. There were a lot of rumors going around about him, that he was corrupt and dug up dirt on people to control them. He didn't know if they were true or not. He did know he didn't like the man, and the less he had to do with him, the better. But he was the man in charge over here, so whether he liked him or not, he had to try to work with him.

They pulled into and parked at the Ellis County Courthouse. Getting out, he looked up at the old Courthouse. It was beautiful. The three men standing together just stared at it. "Can you imagine what it took to build this?" Carter said. Carter walked over to the historical marker. It was constructed in 1897 by J. Riely Gordon. Romanesque Revival Style. With arched entrances on each side facing true north, south, east, and west. Built with red and gray stone. In the center was a tall clock tower with a Roman numeral clock on each side.

Carter turned to Hayes. "Hey, Billy, you grew up here, didn't you?" Hayes looks over at Carter. "Yes, as a matter of fact, my great-grandfather worked on the clocks here." "Oh really," Carter said. "Ya, I remember my mother saying he would stick his head up and wave from up there in front of the face of the clock." Both Carter and Roberts smiled. "Wow, that's cool," Roberts said.

Hayes then smiles and turns to them. "Well, if you think that's cool. Have you ever heard of the legend of the Ellis County Courthouse? Carter and Roberts look at each other and then back at Hayes. "No, guess not," Carter says. Hayes turns to face the courthouse. "Well, legend has it that in 1895, when they started working on the courthouse, there was a German stone carver named Harry Herley.

While working here, he met and fell madly in love with a local girl named Mabel Frame. She did not return his love. He carved a beautiful likeness of her face around the door to impress her. As he worked his way around the courthouse, he did more carving of her. As his love dwindled, the carving became more ugly until he came to the last door, and her likeness is the most hideous." Carter and Robert look at Hayes with a surprised look on their face. "Really," Carter says. "I have never heard that." Hayes turns back to them. "Well, this is a legend, so there may or may not be any truth to it. But there is one more twist to the story you might be interested in.

Carter and Roberts follow Hayes around to the south side of the building. Hayes looks up higher and says. "He made one last carving." As the three men stand to stare at the courthouse. An older woman with glasses and black hair covered in a black scarf, carrying a huge black purse, walks up. She stops when she gets to the men. She says. "I think what you are looking for is right up there to the right of the window." She points. They take a hard look. "Is that what I think it is?" Carter says Roberts looks back at him. "It can't be." They both turn and look at the old woman. "I'm old but not that old. I just know that I work across the street and see people come and stare up there."

Hayes walks over to the woman. "Ms. Tyler, how are you doing. Do you remember me? She smiles. "Of course, I do your Billy Hayes, Fran's boy." He smiles and gives her a hug." "How have you been?" Hayes says. "I have been doing good," she says. Hayes turns to Carter and Roberts. "This is Ms. Tyler. I have known her for most of my life. Carter and Roberts shake hands with her. "Nice to meet you, Ms. Tyler." They both say. She turns and hugs Hayes again. "I've got to go. I'm running late. You know me. I'll be late for my own funeral. She waves and starts walking off. She turns and says. "I know your Mother is proud of you, Billy. So am I." Hayes waves back. "Thank you."

Hayes walks back over to where Carter and Roberts are still looking at the courthouse. They all look at each other. Carter says, "Well, if that is what it looks like, he must have known her really well."

Carter grew a little uneasy. He could smell the cigar smoke before he heard the voice. "Tell me you didn't get me up here on my day off to talk about an old wise tale!" Carter turns around to see Sheriff Jack Truman standing behind him. He stood about 5 foot 10 with a round belly and balding hair under a straw cowboy hat. "Hello, Sheriff Truman, thank you for coming." Truman took the cigar out of his mouth. "Forget about thanking me. Just get to why the hell you are here? Carter handed Truman the file on Captain Briggs. "Sheriff, we believe that a man we have been looking for is here in Ellis County, and we think he may be here to kill Captain Briggs. We wanted to talk to you as a courtesy and see if you wanted to come with us to talk to Captain Briggs." Truman looks through the file. "This is just a file on this Capitan fucker. What makes you think somebody is going to kill him?" Carter takes the file back from Truman. "We recovered this file from a car the suspect was driving." Truman takes a hard drag from his cigar. "That doesn't mean he is going to kill him." Carter shakes his head. "The man is wanted in connection with the murders in Limestone County." Truman blows smoke toward Carter. "Oh, you mean the guy you let run around your County killing people. Then you let him burn down a landmark. Oh, and then you let him get away! That Man?" Carter takes a moment to let his anger die down. "Yes, that man," Truman chomped down hard on his cigar and takes it out of his mouth. "Look, Carter, you really fucked things up in your county and if you think I'm going to let you spill your shit over into my county, you got another thing coming. I don't even want to be seen talking to you. I'm up for re-election this year, too. I don't want to get your stink on me. You need to get your ass back in that car and go back to that shithole County of yours. Truman turns and walks back to his car and gets in.

Carter, Roberts, and Hayes watch him drive away. Roberts looks over at Carter. "So what are we going to do, boss?" Carter turns to face Roberts and Hayes. "Well, we didn't come here to turn back now. Let's go find Briggs."

*

Slone made the drive out to Briggs's place. He parked about a half-mile away. He hid the car as best he could. He didn't want the Russians to see it and get spooked. He would walk the rest of the way.

Taking his rifle out of the trunk, he quickly put it together. He made his way through the woods till he could see the clearing behind Briggs cabin. He found a spot high with lots of cover. It would work perfectly. It would be about a 150-meter shot, which would be very easy for a man with his skill set. He looked through the scope and looked around the target area and its surroundings. He would take out Briggs first, then the 1st Russian doing the talking. The 2nd Russian would be standing back, looking around. They would be nervous that Briggs would double-cross them. But there was no real cover for him to get to. He would have to hurry to get him before he could return fire. Now all he had to do was wait. That was always the hardest part.

About 20 minutes later, Slone saw movement at the back of the cabin. He looked through his scope and saw Captain Briggs coming out of the back door and out onto the back porch. He watched as Briggs looked around and then looked at his watch. It was going down soon. Slone looked around through his scope. He didn't see anything yet. He came back to Briggs. He was coming down off the porch into the back yard. Again, he looked around and then back at his watch.

After about 10 minutes of Briggs nervously looking around, Slone saw movement at the edge of the woods behind the cabin. He saw two men. Looking at them through the scope, he could see they were the same men he had seen at the restaurant in Dallas. He watched as they cautiously walked up. They had probably been watching Briggs from the woods. They would be fearful of Briggs double-crossing them. One of the men carried a large backpack. It most likely had the money in it.

Briggs walked toward them. They stopped about 5 meters apart. They said something to each other. One of the Russians held up the bag and opened it to show Briggs what was inside. Briggs then reached into his pocket, pulled something out, and held it up. Most likely, it was a microchip with the information on it.

They then walked closer to make the exchange. This would be his chance. He put the crosshairs right on Briggs' head. Just as he was reaching for the money, he pulled the trigger. He saw Briggs' head snap back. He chambered another round, he found the Russian with the bag, and fired just as he was starting to react to the first shot, hitting him in the side of the head. He then chambers a third round and finds the 2nd Russian fully turning now, drawing his weapon. He fired, hitting him squire in the chest.

There was silence for a moment, as he looked through the scope, he looked over at each of the three men. They were all dead. He picked up his shell casings. Now he just had to retrieve the microchip and then clean up. He stood up, slung the rifle over his shoulder, and started making his way down there.

*

Carter, Roberts, and Hayes pulled up in front of Captain Briggs cabin. They were just getting out when they heard the quick shots. They quickly looked at each other and then drew their weapons as they started moving around the cabin to the back. Carter stopped on the side of the porch. He peeked around and saw the three men lying on the ground. Carter then looked around the area. He saw Slone with a rifle coming toward them. But just as he saw Slone, Slone saw him, turned, and started running.

Carter shouted to Hayes. "Check them," pointing to the bodies. He then turned to Roberts and threw him his car keys. "Get the car!"

Carter then started running toward Slone, who had at least a 50-yard head start.

He ran through the woods as fast as he could. He could no longer see Slone but could hear him running. He heard a car start. He came out of the woods onto the road just in time to see the car speed away. He aimed his 38 pistol at it and fired, mostly out of frustration rather than any hope of stopping it.

A minute or so later, Roberts pulls up in the patrol car. Carter jumps in. "He went that way," pointing down the road. Roberts hits the gas, and they take off. About a mile down the road, they come to a crossroads. They stop. Roberts turns to Carter. "Which way?" Carter pauses for a moment. Then he remembers. "He is in the same car I put a tracker on in Tulsa. Could it still be working?" Roberts nods. "Yes, assuming the battery is still up." Carter gets on the computer in the car and checks. "Yes, we are still getting a signal. Turn left." They turned left and headed down the road.

*

Slone didn't see anybody following him. He had made several turns, so he was sure he had lost them. He pulled into a gas station. How had Carter found him? He asks himself. He got out of the car. He felt up under the wheel well of the car. He found it. A tracker, Carter, must have put it on the car when he was following his mother. He walked over and put it on the bumper of a car that was leaving. He waited a few minutes and saw a Limestone County patrol car come speeding by.

Okay, he had to get out of here before they found out they were following the wrong car. He got in the car and headed out in the other direction. He needed to ditch this car, and somehow, some way, he had to get that microchip back.

Chapter 14

Carter and Roberts drove back up to Captain Briggs cabin. They had lost him. Slone had obviously found the tracker and put it on another car, sending them on a wild goose chase following the wrong car.

Getting out, they walked around to the back and found Deputy Hayes taking pictures of the crime scene. Hayes turned to them. "Have any luck?" Hayes said. Carter looked down with a disgusted look on his face. "No the son of a bitch got away again! Have you called anybody yet?" "No," Hayes said. "I was waiting for you to get back." Carter paused for a moment, then turned to Roberts. "Call the Ellis County Sheriff's office and get them to come out. This is their jurisdiction, so they need to be out here. I just hope to hell Sheriff Truman doesn't come out with them. I'm not in the mood for his mouth.

Roberts stepped away to make the call. Carter looked around. He wanted to get a good look at things before they got here. The man shot in the head he recognized from the file picture as Captain Briggs. The other two men, both white male,s one shot in the head, the other in the chest. The man shot in the chest must have been shot last. He had his gun in his hand. He had time to react. There was a bag of money lying on the ground next to the other guy. He took out some latex gloves and put them on. He went through the two men's pockets. No ID. He was willing to bet their fingerprints would not be in the system. He looked over at Captain Briggs if these guys were trying to give Briggs money. What were they getting in return? He reached down and opened up Briggs's hand. Inside was a microchip. Oh wow. They were buying this. What could be on a microchip that a Captain in the Navy was selling?

Roberts walks up. "Sheriff Truman is on his way. He is not happy." Carter rolls his eyes. He holds up the microchip. "I found this in Briggs's hand. A bag of money on the ground. Briggs was selling this to them if it was just Slone's job to kill them. Why would he be coming down here? Why not just take off?" Roberts looks back towards where Slone came. "He wouldn't," Roberts said. "Right," Carter says. "Unless he was after something. I'm betting it was this!" Carter holds the microchip up." Roberts looks at the microchip. "What do you think is on it?" Carter shakes his head. "I don't know, and we are probably better off not knowing.

Hayes walks over closer to them. "So what are we going to do, Boss?" Hayes says. Carter looks over at both of them. "Whatever is on this. Slone wants it. Maybe it will lead us to him."

Roberts looks over at them. "Sheriff Truman will be here any minute. It will be evidence. We will never see it again." Carter looks over at them. "The first thing he will do is run us off or arrest us. That bag of money will make its way into his re-election fund." Roberts and Hayes looked at each other and then back at Carter. "So what are we going to do?" Roberts asks. Carter looks at the microchip and over at them. "Only one thing to do." Carter puts the microchip in his mouth and swallows it.

Roberts and Hayes's eyes get big, and they look at Carter. Roberts says. "Oh my gosh, John! What are you doing?" Carter keeps swallowing hard, trying to get it down. Then says. "It's the only way to keep it out of Truman's hands."

A few minutes later, they hear the cars pull up. A few moments later, Sheriff Jack Truman comes walking around the house. He was short and stocky, overweight. He had a straw cowboy hat pulled down low and a cigar in his mouth. A stream of smoke followed him like a smokestack on an old freight train. When he got to, he took a hard look at Carter, then over at Roberts and Hayes, and then back to Carter. He took a drag off the cigar and then took it out of his mouth. Then he says. "Just what the fuck do you think you are doing? I told you to get the fuck out of my County and back to your shithole. Now I find you here. In my County, with three dead bodies!" Carter looks over at the bodies. his deputies have started taking pictures, and the man that must be the medical examiner is looking at the bodies. He looks back at Truman. "We told you that Captain Briggs life might be in danger. We gave you the chance to come with us. You really didn't think we would just turn around and go home, did you?" Truman bites down hard on his cigar. "When I tell people to get out of my County! They get out of my County!"

Truman then walks over to the medical examiner. He takes the cigar out of his mouth. "So, Doc, what can you tell me?" The Doctor looked up at him. "Looks like these two died from gunshot wounds to the head, the other took one to the chest." Truman looks down on him and frowns. "No shit Doc. Tell me something I don't already know." The doctor looks back at him. "It's going to take some time, Sheriff. When I know more, you will know more."

Truman walks back over to Carter. Carter points in the direction of the hill and the woods. "The shots came from up there someplace." Truman snaps his head around. "I don't need any fucking help from you! He then turns and yells. "Fields." Deputy Fields comes running up. "Yes, Sheriff." Truman points over to Carter, Roberts, and Hayes. "I think you know Sheriff Carter and his two sidekicks." Fields looks at them and smiles. "Yes, I know Sheriff Carter and Dupites Roberts and Hayes." "Good," Truman says. "I want you to search them and their car. They have a file on Captain Briggs, get it. Take their weapons and give them a ride down to the office. Put them in an interrogation room."

Carter, Roberts, and Hayes look at each other but say nothing as Fields pats them down and takes their side arms. When Fields runs his hand down Carter's leg, he feels something. "What's that?" he asks. Carter pulls his pants leg up and reveals an ankle holster with a small 9mm in it. Carter takes it out and hands it to Fields. "Thank you, Sheriff," Fields said as they started walking up the hill.

When they get to the car, Carter gives Fields the file on Briggs. "Thank you." Fields said. "I'm sorry about the way Sheriff Truman has treated you." Carter smiled. "That's just Truman being himself. Asshole all the way through." Fields laffed. "You got that right. You know I enjoyed my time working with you. You will always have my utmost respect." Carter nodded and said. "I would tell you could come to work for us anytime. But with the election coming up, I might not have a job very long.

They got in their cars and drove back to the Sheriff Department. Deputy Fields led them to the conference room. Carter sits down. "Ya know Truman said the interrogation room," Carter says. Fields smiles. "I know. This will do. Can I get you anything?" "No," Carter says. "But if there is any info on the two John Doe, I would appreciate it." Fields nods. "Will do," he says as he leaves the room. Hayes and Roberts set down. "So what now, boss?" Hayes says. Carter stands up and looks out the window. "We do what we can do. Wait."

About an hour later, Fields comes back in and brings them each a bottle of water. "Thanks," Carter says. Fields sits down with them. "The only body that had any ID on it was Captain Briggs. The other two had nothing on them. There was one interesting thing. He pulls up a picture on his phone and shows it to Carter. "One of them had a tattoo, and it had some foreign language in it." Carter looks at it. "That's Russian," he says. Fields shows Roberts and Hayes. "That's what I thought, too." Fields says. Fields stands up. "Truman's on his way back, so it won't be much longer. "Thank you, Mike," Carter says. "Anytime, Sheriff." Fields says as he leaves the room.

About 30 minutes later, they heard a loud voice say. "Where the hell are they?" A few moments later, Sheriff Truman walks in. He looks at Carter and says. "I have spent the last two hours cleaning up your fucking mess! So let me get this straight. You get a lead that the guy who did all the killing up in your County is coming down here to kill this Captain. Did you try to warn him?" Truman takes a hard look at Carter. "Yes," Carter says. "We tried several times, and his people blew us off." Truman takes out a cigar and lights it right under the no-smoking sign. Truman takes a deep drag off the cigar. "Everything you had on this guy is in that file? "Yes," Carter says. Truman pauses for a moment and then takes the cigar out of his mouth. "Ok, here is what's going to go down. I want the three of you out of my County. I won't mention your names in any of my reports, and as far as anybody knows, you were never here. Just so you know. I'm not doing this as any kind of favor to you. I don't want your stink on me! Have I made myself absolutely clear? Carter nods his head. "Yes, very clear, Sheriff." "Good," Truman says.

Then he shouts. "Fields!" A moment later, Deputy Fields comes in. Truman turns to him. "Give them their stuff back and get them the hell out of here." "Yes, sir." Fields said.

About 15 minutes later, Carter, Roberts, and Hayes walk out of the Ellis County Sheriff's Department. Getting into their patrol car, they make the hour-long drive back to Groesbeck in mostly silence. They know that they missed out on maybe their last chance to catch this guy. It's about 8:30 p.m. when they pull into the Sheriff's office parking lot.

Roberts and Hayes go straight to their cars, and Carter goes inside to see how things are going. Carter briefly talks to the staff on duty and then goes to his office. He picks up the phone and calls Carolyn. He talks to her and the kids for a few minutes. With them staying at her mother's, there is no hurry to get home. He sits back in his chair. What the hell was he going to do now? Not much he can do till that microchip passes through his body. He was already regretting that move. He looked up the info online. It would take at least 24 hours. So nothing was going to happen with that tonight.

He gathered up everything they had on Slone and took it to the conference room. He might as well get something done while he waited.

*

Jake Slone had driven his mother's car out on the back roads of Ellis County. He had to get rid of it. It was too well known now. He had gotten a five-gallon can of gasoline and poured it all over the inside and outside of the car. He had called Nathan Hunter to come and pick him up. As soon as Hunter got there, Slone lit a match and threw it down, engulfing the car in flames. He got into the car with Hunter and drove off.

Slone had already filled Hunter in on what had happened over the phone. Hunter looked over at him. "With the targets eliminated, we can still salvage the op. But we have to get that microchip back." Hunter hands Slone a file. "This is what we have on the Ellis County Sheriff, Jack Truman. The FBI has a file on him. They are certain he is dirty, but he is good at covering his tracks, and they can't prove anything. But he doesn't know that. I think we can bluff him into doing everything we want and get the microchip back. I'm going to go see him in the morning." Slone nods. "Ok, I will go with you." Hunter shakes his head. "No. Carter no doubt shared a picture of you with him. We can't take a chance on you getting made." "Ya, you are right," Slone said.

They drove back to Red Oak, a small town just north of Waxahachie, and got a motel room. The next morning, they got up, got ready, and drove back into Waxahachie. Hunter pulled up outside the Sheriff's Office. He reached inside his pocket and pulled out an FBI badge and credentials. He was now FBI Special Agent Alan Green. Putting it back in his suit pocket, he looked over at Slone. "This shouldn't take long," Hunter said. "Slone nods. "I'll be here."

He picks up the file on Truman and gets out and walks inside. Hunter looked around. It looked like every Sheriff's Department he had ever been in. Deputies sitting at desks, walking around. A woman at the front desk looked up at him. "Can I help you?" She asks. He walked over to her, pulled out his badge, and showing it to her. "I'm Special Agent Alan Green with the FBI. I need to speak to Sheriff Jack Truman. It's urgent." She got up and walked into an office that must be

Truman's. A moment later, she walked back out and up to him. "You can go right in. Can I get you some coffee?" He smiled at her. "No, thank you."

He then walked through the door into Truman's office. He saw a short overweight, balding man, fifty or so sitting behind the desk, a half-smoked and unlit cigar in his mouth. Truman looked at him with a frown on his face. Hunter reached into his suit pocket and pulled out his badge. "I'm Special Agent Alan Green with the FBI." Truman takes the cigar out of his mouth and says. "I'm a busy man! So cut to the chase, what do you want?" Hunter nods. "Sheriff, I believe yesterday you were called to the scene of a triple murder involving Captain Marvin Briggs. I need you to stop that investigation. Label Captain Briggs' death a suicide and turn over the other two bodies and all the evidence to me. It's a matter of national security."

Truman looks up at him with disbelief in his eyes. "You gotta be fucking kidding me!" Truman says in an elevated voice. Hunter shakes his head. "No, I'm afraid not, Sheriff." Truman puts the cigar back in his mouth, stands up, lights it, and blows smoke toward Hunter. "Look special agent prick FBI fucker. I got a press conference in about an hour, and I'm going to tell the world that Captain Briggs was murdered along with two other unknown people, and it happened in Ellis County, and I'm working the case alone! So you can take your little FBI ass and get it out of my office." Truman then puts the cigar back in his mouth and looks down at the papers he has on his desk. A few moments later, he looks back up at Hunter. "Why the fuck are you still here?"

"Well, Sheriff," Hunter says. "I was hoping we could do this the easy way, but I guess we can't." Hunter then opens his file and puts it in front of Truman." Truman looks down at it. "What the fuck is this?" He says, looking up at Hunter. "It's an FBI file we have on you, Sheriff. There is a lot of stuff in there. Stuff I'm sure you would not want to get out." Truman's face gets red with anger. "You assholes have been investigating me!" "Yes," Hunter says. "For quite some time." Truman closes the file. "If you could prove any of this, you would have acted on it a long time ago," Truman says. Hunter picks up his file. "Maybe so," Hunter says. "But we have more than enough for an indictment. You will at the very least be suspended while all this comes out. A lot of people will be pissed off and there is an election coming up. You could lose your job and lose your hold on the people in power in Ellis County. At that point, going to jail might look good. So what's it going to be, Sheriff?

Truman takes a deep drag off the cigar. "Ok Mr. FBI fucker. I guess we have a deal!" Hunter smiles. "I thought you would see it my way. I will send a van over to pick up the two bodies of the two unknown men. If you will get everything else together for me, pictures, the whole works, and most importantly. The microchip you recovered, I need that in my hand right now."

Truman frowns. "We didn't recover any microchip! Hunter turns sharply. "What do you mean you didn't recover a microchip. It would have been very obvious!" Truman walks around his desk. "I meant just what I fucking said. We didn't recover any microchip!" He pauses for a moment. "Carter," Truman says. "That fucking prick Carter. He must have taken it before we got there." Hunter feels his anger rise. "You're telling me, Sheriff, that a vital piece of national security is missing?" Truman turns and says. "Limestone County Sheriff John Carter has it." Truman then grabs his phone off his desk. "I'll get the little prick on the phone." As Truman starts to dial, Hunter pushes the button, hanging up the phone. "Don't Sheriff, I will take care of Carter. Get everything you have together. I will send my people to pick everything up, including the bodies." Hunter turns and heads for the door. he stops and turns back. "That news conference, cancel it.

Hunter hurries out to the car and gets in. Slone says. "How did it go?" "Carter has the microchip," Hunter said. Slone turns to face him. "Oh shit!" he said. After a brief pause, Hunter says. "I put together a file on Carter, too. He is squeaky clean. So we won't have any leverage on him as we did on Truman." Slone looks out the window. "I guess I will be heading back to Groesbeck."

Chapter 15

When Carter heard his alarm going off, he abruptly opened his eyes. Momentarily confused as to where he was, he then realized that he had fallen asleep on the couch in his office. He set up and rubbed his face. He had not intended to spend the whole night here. He got up and returned to the conference room where he had been working.

He had everything up on a rolling pegboard. Pictures of all the major players. Its looked good. He was going to call the FBI this afternoon and give them an update on the events of the last few weeks. Then there was the matter that damn microchip that he has swallowed. Hopefully, that would literally work itself out sometime today.

A few minutes later, he heard the door open and looked up to see Nancy walk in. "Have you been here all night?" Nancy said. "Carter nodded. "Yes, I have." She gives him a hard look. "John can't do this to yourself. You're going to let this job kill you." Carter pulled out a chair and sat down at the table. "Well, if we don't catch this guy, I won't have to worry about the job killing me. I won't have one." She shakes her head but says nothing. "Well, I will get you some coffee going." She said as she walked out of the conference room. "Thank you, Nancy," Carter said. He couldn't help but chuckle. If he somehow caught this guy and kept his job. Nancy's coffee might kill him.

A few minutes later, Nancy walks back in with a cup of coffee and hands it to him. She is followed through the door by Deputy Roberts and Hayes. Hayes looks at the peg board and says, "Wow, you must have been here all night." Carter walks over beside them. "Ya, I was." They all three stairs at the board for a few minutes, and then Carter says, "Let's just go over this one more time."

Hayes and Roberts pull out chairs and sit down, while Carter stands by the board. "It all starts with Doyle McKinney, a wealthy

Limestone County fatcat. According to his son, Mike, McKinney wanted a high-profile ambassadorship with the correct administration. Congress had blocked money going into Afghanistan to help fight the Taliban and later I,SIS so he couldn't just give them his money. So the CIA devised this plan to grow and produce drugs to raise money off the books to send over there. McKinney agreed to do this to gain favor with the administration in the hope of becoming an ambassador. He was told law enforcement would look the other way." Roberts laffs. "He was told wrong." Carter smiles. "He should have known better than that." Carter turns back to the board. "He gets this up and running with his son Mike McKinney running the show.

After a while, we start to get suspicious about the new flow of drugs in Limestone County. We suspect the McKinneys but can't prove anything. They know all law enforcement in Limestone and Freestone Counties, so I bring in Mike Fields from Ellis County to go undercover. We get the goods and arrest Mike McKinney, but don't get anything linking Doyle McKinney to It. Mike won't turn on his father and takes the fall for all of it.

Doyle McKinney is outraged. He didn't get the protection he was promised. Now, with his reputation ruined and his son in jail. McKinney goes rogue. He uses his CIA connections to hire a hitman to take out everybody who had anything to do with his son's conviction. That's when the killings start." Carter moves over and points to the pictures of the victims.

"James Johnson, Sam Logan, Pam Smith, Stanley Cox, Mary Anderson, Tim Baker, Fred Freeman, and Chris Young all had been either a Judge, or prosecutor, or on the jury. He also shot a Mart policeman and a Mexia Game Warden, Jeff Fisk. But went to a lot of trouble not to kill them."

Roberts looks over at Carter and says. "That's something that has always bothered me. Why didn't he kill them? It would have been easier on him. No witnesses." Carter turns around. "I don't know. Maybe some killer code. You only kill people you're paid to kill."

Carter turns back to the board. "Then we catch a break and raid his motel room, we just miss him but get some info that leads us to believe that his next victim is Charles Lewis, who works out at Fort Parker. We find out that Lewis is already at work, we head out there to find that our killer has taken hostages and is holding up in the fort. We surround him and negotiate for the hostages. After sending the kids out, he sets the fort on fire and escapes through an old tunnel we didn't know existed. Later that night, I get a phone call from Doyle McKinney's cell phone from the killer, telling me he and Mr. McKinney have finished their business and that it was over. We headed over to McKinney's place and find him dead. There must have been some kind of falling out, and the killer turned on McKinney. That's where the trail went cold."

Carter takes a long look at all the pictures on the board."Then, a few months later, we go back to Mike McKinney, whose father has died and his money is drying up while he is in prison. We get him to let us in on his father's CIA connections. He lets us search Doyle McKinney's cabin, where he kept all his files. There we find the file on Jake Slone, a highly decorated Navy SEAL who was killed in Afghanistan 10 years ago. We ID him as our killer. I go to Tusla to talk to his mother. Go by and see local Sheriff Jim Dorsey first. I found out that Dorsey knows Slone, served together in the Navy. He tells me he is dead and to go home. I go see his mother anyway. She tells me he is dead. I feel like she knows more than what she is telling. I find out that Slone has a daughter that is sick Heart problems. I put a tracker on his mother's car. Sure enough, she leads me to him. He flees in her car, I follow and get hit going through a red light by a truck. Slone comes and pulls me out of the car. Passing up the chance to kill me. He then gets away. I come home empty-handed with a wrecked patrol car."

Carter stops for a moment and sits down. This is the point that things with Carolyn had gotten to the edge of the breaking point. He was overcome with grief. This was the real reason he had not gone home last night. He had to pull himself together. He couldn't lose it in front of Roberts and Hayes. About that time, Roberts says. "You ok, boss?" Carter turns to him and smiles. "Yes, I'm sorry. No sleep."

Turning back to the board, Carter continued. "The next day, after I get home, I'm attacked in my home. A man later identified as Jeff Spencer tried to kill me and make it look like a suicide. If not for my kids coming home when they did, he would have succeeded." Carter stopped again. This is what pushed Carolyn to the breaking point. He couldn't think about that now. "We arrest him and he lawyers up and then commits suicide in our jail.

Just when we think our last lead is gone, Tulsa County Sheriff Jim Dorsey shows up and gives me a file he found in Slone's truck. It is a detailed file on Captain Marvin Briggs. He thinks that Slone is going to kill Captain Briggs. We try to contact Briggs's office, and he is gone for the weekend, and his staff blows us off. We head to his Ellis County place after talking to Ellis County Sheriff Jack Truman, who declines to help us. As we get there, we hear three shots. Coming around to the back, we find three bodies, including Captain Briggs. We spot Slone coming toward us, he sees us and flees. We chase him. At some point, he finds the tracker we have in his car, puts it in another car, and sends us on a wild goose chase. We return to the house and find a bag of cash and a microchip in Briggs' hand. We call Sheriff Truman. But first, I swallow the microchip to prevent Truman from finding it. I didn't feel like he could be trusted with it."

Carter stops, turns around, and holds his stomach. "I will never do that again," Roberts smiles. So, how is that project coming, boss?" Carter frowns. Nothing yet, but I hope soon."

Turning back to the board. "Ok, finishing up. We think that Briggs was selling secrets to the Russians. One of the dead men had a Russian tattoo. Ok, I guess that's where we are at. Y'all have anything to add?" Roberts shakes his head. "I think you covered it all." He said. Hayes looks over at them and says. "So where do we go from here?" There was a long pause, then Carter said. "I guess we call the FBI. We show them this." He points to the board. "Tell them everything and turn over the microchip." Roberts and Hayes look at each other and then back at Carter, and Roberts says. "So that's it for us? We let them take it?" "Yes," Carter says. "I think we have screwed this up enough." Carter starts walking toward the door, and stops, and turns back to them. "I'm heading home for a while and going to try to get the microchip problem solved. Call if you need anything.

Carter made his way out to his car and made the drive home. He was starting to have some pain in his lower body. He hoped that was a good sign that this was coming to an end. Oh boy, did he regret doing this! What was he thinking? As he unlocked the door and entered the house, he couldn't help but notice the overwhelming quiet. No, Carolyn, no kids. Then he realized. They would not be home this time of day anyway. He felt better for a moment, but then his next thought. They probably wouldn't be home anytime soon. So now he was back to being bummed. He had to stop doing this to himself.

He took his gun belt off and put it on the table in the entryway. Not something he would normally do. He always put it in the gun safe. But this was not a normal day. He put his cowboy hat on the hat rack and he went straight through the bedroom to the bathroom. Let's try to get this over with.

About 30 minutes later, he came out. He looked at a small package with the microchip in it. It didn't look any worse for the ware. He had cleaned it up. The super small zip-lock bag it had been in had protected it. He was never doing this again. His stomach still felt upset. How do people do this all the time?

He walked back through the bedroom and back into the hallway when he was startled by what he saw. Jake Slone standing there with a gun pointed at him. Carter's right hand instinctively reaches for his gun that's not there. "Hello, John," Slone says. They momentarily stare at each other. "How did you get in here?" Carter says. Slone smiles. "You really didn't think that lock on the door was going to stop me, did you?" Slone looks at that microchip in Carter's hand. "I think that is what I have come for." He holds out his hand, and Carter hands it to him." Slone looks at it and smiles. "How did you sneak this out?" Carter looks back at him. "I swallowed it!" Slone frowns. "John! You couldn't have told me that before you handed it to me."

Slone motions for Carter to move. They walked through the living room to the kitchen table. Slone says. "You're not going to offer me something to drink, John? Ya know it was hot outside waiting for you." Carter turns to the fridge, opens it up, gets out a bottle of water, and puts it on the table. "Thank you, John. Please sit down." Carter pulls out a chair and sits down as dose Slone." Slone opens the bottle of water and takes a drink. Carter looks over at him. "So what was this all about? Why did you kill Captain Briggs? Slone shakes his head. "I'm sorry I can't get into that, John. You're a smart guy. I'm sure you have put it together by now." Carter looks back at Slone. "Well, I know Captain Briggs was disgruntled. I know one of the dead men was a Russian by his tattoo. So, putting two and two together along with the microchip. I would say Briggs was selling secrets to the Russians. What I don't know is. Who you're going to sell that microchip to?" Slone lays the microchip out on the table. He looks over at Carter and says. "Oh, I'm not going to sell it to anybody," Carter smirks. "Ya right," He says. Slone then pulls his gun over the table and takes the butt of his gun and smashes the microchip. Slone then looks at Carter. "Satisfied now, John?" Carter stares at it in disbelief. Slone then says. "I don't want to sell it. I just don't want it falling into the wrong hands."

Carter looks at Slone from across the table. "So what now? Are you going to kill me?" Slone smiles. "Oh, John. If I wanted to kill you, I could have done it long before now. But here is the deal. The Briggs killing will be ruled a suicide. He was depressed about his upcoming discharge from the Navy." Slone said. Carter frowns. "There is no way you will get Sheriff Truman to go along with that!" Slone shakes his head. "I already got that covered. It seems that Sheriff Truman was convinced it was in his best interest. "Oh," Carter says. "You have something on him." Slone smiles. "Let's just say he was easier to work with than you."

About that time, the doorbell ring,s followed by a knock on the door. Slone wipes his head around. "Who is that?" "I don't know," Carter says. Slone then pulls his gun up and says. "Look, I don't want to hurt anybody. But I will if I have to. Get rid of them."

They both get up, and Carter leads the way to the front door. He looks through the small window. "It's my brother." Slone stands behind the door. "Get rid of him or I will." Carter reaches for the doorknob and opens the door. "Hey, Brother," Carter says. Brian smiles. "Hey," Brian says. " You, Carolyn, and the kids weren't at church yesterday. "I saw your car. I just wanted to check and make sure y'all were doing ok." Carter smiles. "Ya oh, Carolyn and the kids have been really sick, some kind of virus. I would ask you to come in, but I don't want to expose you to it. They're at the doctor now." Brian nods. "Wow, I see. I hope they get to feeling better. I will pray for them. I will come by later and check on them. You feeling ok?" Carter nods. "Ya, I'm fine." "Good," Brian says. "I will come by later and check on them." Brian steps back away from the door. Carter says. "I will see you at service on Wednesday. Oh, Bria,n our Bible verse for Wednesdays is Hebrews 13:3, right? Brian turns and looks at Carter. "Yes, that's right." Carter smiles. "I'd better look over it. Talk to you later." Carter closes the door and looks at Slone. "Good," Slone says. He then motions with his gun to go back to the kitchen.

As they walk back to the kitchen table. Carter decides he has to make a move. He balls up his right fist tight and turns and swings hard, landing on the unsuspecting Slone's jaw, staggering him back and dropping his gun. Carter follows up with a left that Slone blocks, and he then counters with a hard left to Carter's face. A dazed Carter takes a wild swing, missing badly. Slone hits Carter hard with a right to the body, slumping Carter over. Slone then grabs Carter by the hair of his head and then comes up hard with a knee to the face. Sending Carter to the floor, where he loses consciousness.

Slone then picks up his gun and walks over to Carter and looks down at him. "You just can't do anything the easy way, can you, John?" Slone turns around and is startled by what he sees. Brian Carter pointing his brother's gun at him. Slone looks at him and says. "Well, you must be the brother?" Brian looks back, "Yes. Now drop the gun and put your hands on your head." Slone smiles and walks two steps closer to Brian. "You know, in my line of work. You learn to read people by looking into their eyes. You get the feeling when someone will shoot and when they won't, and looking into your eyes. You won't." He turns around and looks at Carter on the floor. "Your brother is not hurt bad. I think I will just be on my way." He takes a step toward the door. Brian cocks the gun. "This is my Papaw's gun. I can assure you he taught me how to use it." Slone looks over at him and says. "Oh, I'm sure he did. But we both know you're not going to."

Slone takes two more steps toward the door when a shot rings out. Slone falls to the floor, shot in the shoulder. Brian looks around and sees his brother holding his 9mm that he had in his ankle holster. Carter gets up, wipes the blood from his nose, and walks over to Slone and kicks his gun away. He looks over at Brian. "You ok?" Brian nods. "Get my handcuffs off my gun belt on the table." Brian goes and does this and comes back. Carter looks at him. "Cuff him." Brian looks down at Slone on the floor in pain. "He is bleeding, John!" Carter nods. "Cuff him and call an ambulance," Carter says. Brian does this and calls 911.

Carter puts his gun away, walks and gets some kitchen towels, and comes back to Slone and applies pressure to the gunshot wound. Slone looks up at him. Carter says. "If you had looked into my eyes, you would have seen I have no problem shooting you. Slone forced a smile in his pain. "I will remember that, John."

The ambulance showed up along with deputies Roberts and Hayes. Carter looks at them. "I want both of you to go with him to the hospital and check his clothes and boots for anything he might use to kill himself. Don't let him out of your sight. They put Slone on a stretcher and wheeled him out with Roberts and Hayes close behind.

Carter walks over to Brian. "I guess you picked up on my Hebrews 13:3 reference. I was hoping I was remembering it right." Brian smiles. "Ya, I got it. Hebrews 13:3 Continue to remember those in prison as if you were together with them in prison and those who are mistreated as if you yourselves were suffering." Brian smiles. "I'm impressed brother." Carter wipes the blood from his nose again. "I just intended for you to call for help. Not get involved yourself." Brian hands Carter another towel for his nose. "I did that. But didn't think it could wait." "Well, thank you," Carter says. Brian nods and smiles. "And thank you, John." Carter looks over at him. "For what?" Carter says. Brian looks back. "For not making me find out if I would shoot or not." They look at each other for a moment. Then Brian says. "Let's get that nose looked at." He grabs his brother by the arm and they walk toward the door.

Chapter 16

John Carter heard his alarm go off and quickly turned it off. He lay there momentarily confused. He felt for Carolyn in the bed. She was not there. Then he felt the pain in his face and nose, and it all came back. Had everything that had happened in the last few days really happened. Why couldn't it just be a bad dream, and he could hit the snooze button and cuddle up with Carolyn? No, it had all been real. Well, at least they had the son of a bitch in custody. He sat up. He suddenly felt dizzy. It must be from the concussion that the ER doctor had told him he had.

He got up and made his way to the bathroom, turning on the light, he was shocked to see his reflection in the mirror. He had a thick bandage across his broken nose, both his eyes were black and swollen, and the cut on his head from the car wreck looked red. He looked awful.

He brushed his teeth, shaved, and took a shower. He hoped that it would make him feel better. It didn't. Getting dressed, he thought about what he had to do today. He had called Carolyn last night and told her what had happened. She was upset that he had almost been killed again. He had wanted to go see them last night, but he didn't want them to see him looking like he did last night. Now, this morning, he looked worse.

He called the FBI and updated them on everything that had happened. They were going to contact the Navy and have them pick up Slone and hold him in a secure Navy brig. Technically, Slone was still in the Navy, and killing Captain Briggs also made it a Navy crime. They had assured him that he would return to Limestone County to stand trial for the murders here. It made sense for them to hold him. They were better equipped to handle a dangerous prisoner.

Finishing getting dressed, he put on his gun belt, opened the safe, took out his gun, and checked the load. He heard the front door open. He snapped the 38 together and brought it around in front of him with both hands in the low ready position. He slowly moved to the bedroom door and swung around the corner, bringing his gun up. He quickly lowered it when he saw it was Carolyn.

Carolyn jumped, clearly startled. "Oh my gosh, John! What are you doing?" Carter quickly put his gun away and said. "I'm so sorry. I heard the door, and I was not expecting you." She looks down and then back up at him. "After what happened last night, I thought you would come by Mom's. I was worried about you." Carter walks toward her. "I didn't want you to see me looking like this." He pointed to his black eyes and a broken nose. She reaches up and touches his face and takes a closer look. "You look awful!" Carter nods his head. "Ya, I know."

She takes a step back."Did they give you anything for the pain?" Carter reaches into his pocket and pulls out a bottle of pills. "Yes." She takes the bottle and looks at it. "Have you taken any?" Carter nods. "Yes, I took one last night." She hands the bottle back to him. "Taken any this morning?" "No." He says. "I'm headed to work. Tylenol will have to do." She gives him an angry look. "You're going to work! Are you kidding me! You can barely see, and I'm betting you have a concussion."

Carter paused for a moment. Knowing to choose his words carefully. "I have to go at least for a little while. I have Hayes and Roberts staying with Slone at the hospital. I have to make sure he gets back to the jail and is secure until the Navy picks him up. Then this will all be over."

She looks back at him. "John, you were almost killed for the third time in a few weeks. Our kids could have been killed in our home! A person was shot in our home! Your brother could have been killed! And you almost shot me coming in the door just now! This just can't go away and go back to normal. I have to know our family is safe.

Carter looks at her and starts to speak when his cell phone rings. He looks at it. "It's Roberts from the hospital. I have to take this." She nods. Carter answers the phone. "Carter." He says. "Hey, John. How are you feeling?" Roberts said. "I'm fine," Carter says. "Hey," Roberts says. "There is an NCIS agent here to pick up Slone." "What?" Carter says. "I was not expecting them so soon." "Well," Roberts says. "They are here, and it looks like they got the proper paperwork." Carter pauses for a moment. "Stall them for a few minutes. I'm on my way." "Will do," Roberts says as Carter ends the call.

Carter looks over at Carolyn. "I have to go. Can we get dinner tonight and talk about things?" She nods. "Yes. We can get dinner. I don't know if there is anything to talk about." She turns to walk toward the door. She looks back. "Take care of your business, take your meds, and get some rest." He grabs his cowboy hat off the rack and puts it on his head. "I will, babe," he says as they both walk out the door.

Carter makes the short drive over to the Hospital. He parked his car and quickly made his way to Slone's room number 108. Entering the room, Carter finds deputies Roberts and Hayes talking to a man and two military police officers, placing a belly chain, handcuffs, and leg irons on Slone. He walks up to the man with Hayes and Roberts. Roberts Says. "This is Sheriff Carter." The man turns and shakes hands with Carter. "I'm NCIS agent Alan Green." He pulls out his ID and shows it to Carter. He also hands him the transfer papers. Carter looks over them carefully. Over the years, he had transferred prisoners many times. This all looked in order. Carter looks up. "I really was not expecting you so soon." Agent Green smiles. "Well, we had a team come available this morning, and we didn't want to wait with a man as dangerous as him." Carter nodded and put the papers in his pocket.

Carter turns to Roberts and Hayes. Why don't you guys head back over to the office? I think I might head back home for a little bit. Not feeling so good." "Sure," Roberts says. "You don't look good." As they walk to the door, Hayes says. "Get some rest, boss."

Carter turns around and sees that they have Slone ready to go. He walks over to Slone. "I will see you back here in a few months." Slone smiles. "I underestimated you, John. I'm sorry for the physical and personal toll this has taken on you. You did your job." One of the M.P.'s grabbed him by the arm and led him out the door.

Carter walks over and sits down in a chair by the bed. His head was throbbing. He wanted nothing more than to go home and go back to bed. He sat there for a few minutes. Could this all finally be over? Then it hit him. Oh my god. NCIS agents don't work with the Army Military Police!

He jumps up, fights the dizziness, and runs down the hall to the exit. Going out the exit, he pulls his gun and sees the two M.P.s putting Slone in a van. He points his gun at them and yells. "Stop!" They all turned to look at him. He walks closer and says. "Get down on the ground." About that time, Carter feels a gun stick in his ribs. He turns to see Agent Green. "That's really too bad, Sheriff. Get in the van." Green takes Carter's gun, and they all get in the van.

Inside the van, two bench seats face each other. Carter gets in and faces the front. Agent Green, who is actually Nathan Hunter, sits next to him with his gun facing him. Slone gets in and sits in the chair facing Carter. One M.P. sits next to Slone and removes his cuffs and leg irons, the other drives.

Slone looks over at Hunter. "He has another gun in a boot holster on his left leg. I found out about that one the hard way." Hunter pulls up Carter's pants leg and removes the 9mm from the holster. Slone looks over at Carter. "So what gave us away?" Carter gives him a hard look. "Army M.P.'s don't work for the Navy." Slone turns to Hunter. "That was a careless mistake." Hunter shrugs. "Well, I had to put this plan together on the fly."

They drove a few miles out of town. Hunter yelled up at the driver. "Find a side road and take it." The driver finds a side dirt road and takes it. They drive for about a mile. "This is good enough. Stop here,"

Hunter says. The driver stops, Hunter opens the door, gets out, and says to Carter. "Get out, Sheriff." Carter gets out, as does Slone, and the two M.P.s

Hunter looks over at Carter. "I'm sorry, Sheriff, but you have been a thorn in our side for the last time. Let's go." Hunter directs Carter to move, pointing with his gun. "I'll do it," Slone says. "He is my problem." Hunter looks over at him. "Have it your way." He hands Slone Carter's 38 and 9mm. Slone takes the 38 and puts the 9mm in his belt.

Slone grabs Carter by the arm and pulls him in front of him. "Over there to that dry creek bed." They start walking. Slone says. "You just could not let it go, John! I didn't want to do this. Now you have forced my hand. Carter looks back over his shoulder. "Oh, please. Will you shut the fuck up! The last thing I want to hear is how bad you feel about it. So just do it! Fuck head!"

They got to the dry creek. Slone puts his hand on Carter's shoulder. "Get on your knees," Carter gets down on his knees. Slone reaches down and crosses Carter's feet behind him. He whispers something in Carter's ear. Slone stands back behind Carter, takes aim, and fires a single shot. Carter falls forward face down.

Slone lowers the 38, opens it, and drops all the shells out. He then drops the gun. He turns and takes a few steps toward the van, takes the 9mm out of his belt, drops the clip, and then tosses the gun behind him. He walks back to the van. The others are already inside. He stops for a moment and looks back. He gets in the van and they drive away.

*

Carter lay in the creek bed till he was sure they were gone. He then got up. His ears were ringing. Slone's shot had gone right past his head. Slone had whispered in his ear. Fall forward. So he did. All he could think of now was. Why didn't he kill me? It made no sense. He walked back and picked up his 38 pistol. He didn't bother to try to find the shells. He also picked up his 9mm and walked the mile back to the road. He pulled out his phone. Oh, he didn't want to make this call. He looked like he had one bar of service. He called Deputy Roberts to come and get him.

When Roberts got there, he explained all that had happened. They drove back to the office. He spent the next few hours filling out reports on what had happened, calling the FBI, and explaining it to them.

Deputy Roberts walked into his office. "How are you feeling?" Roberts asks. "Like shit," Carter says. Roberts sits down. "Why don't you go home. Everything has been taken care of." Carter nods. "Did anybody think to get my car from the hospital?" "Yes," Roberts said. "Hayes and I went and got it." "Good." Carter says, "I think I will do that. I'm headed home." Roberts stands up. "Good deal, John. Get some rest."

Carter gets up and heads to the door. He doesn't stop to talk to anybody. He gets in the car and drives home. He really should call Carolyn. But he doesn't know what to say to her. The events of the last few hours would just push her farther away. He just couldn't face that yet. He pulled up in the driveway. He saw some of his re-election signs. He needed to put them back out. But what was the point of that now? Re-election might be hopeless now. But he didn't want to think about that. He walked inside, went to the fridge, and got an Ice pack out of the freezer. He sat down on the couch and put it on his aching head.

At that time, his cell phone rings. He looks at it. It an unknown number. He stares at it for a moment. "Hello, this is Sheriff Carter," he says. "Hello, John." The familiar voice of Jake Slone says. "I'm sorry about how things turned out today. I'm hoping you will take my sparing your life as a gift and just let things go." There was a long pause, then Carter says. "And if you know anything about me. You know that will never happen! One day you will look up and I will be there." There was another long pause, and Slone said. "And if that happens. I will have to kill you, John." Anger grows in Carter as he says. "Or I will kill you!" The line goes dead. Carter tosses the phone down on the coffee table and puts the Ice pack back on his head. Slone turns and tosses his phone in a trash can. He pulls a pair of sunglasses out of his shirt pocket, puts them on, pulls the brim of his baseball cap down low, and turns and walks off.

Author's note

I hope you enjoyed
Murder on a Hitman's Trail
Look for
Murder and Redemption
The last part of the
Carter / Slone trilogy

Other books by Robert D. Coleman

Murder: The John Carter Novels
    Murder and the Cold Case, Book 1
    Murder in Limestone County, Book 2
    Murder on a Hitman's Trail, Book 3
    Murder and Redemption, Book 4
    Murder in the Old West, Book 5
    Murder through a Killer's Eyes, Book 6
    Murder and a Psycho's Revenge, Book 7
    Murder and the Private Detective, Book 8
    Murder in the Shadows, Book 9
    Murder on the Brink of War, Book 10
    Murder and the Long Ride Home, Book 11

Jake Slone: The Man in the Shadows Novels
    Jake Slone: Vengeance is Mine

Don't miss out!

Visit the website below and you can sign up to receive emails whenever Robert D. Coleman publishes a new book. There's no charge and no obligation.

https://books2read.com/r/B-A-ARIGB-WFSAD

BOOKS 2 READ

Connecting independent readers to independent writers.